FISH
TANK

Pre-release reviews

FISH TANK is the ANIMAL FARM for our times. The two books would make a great pair to teach together.

—*Dr. Pete Coppolillo, Ecologist*

[FISH TANK's] message [is] that the self interest of the few can undermine the achievement of a common good....I think FISH TANK could benefit young adults in the same way LORD OF THE FLIES benefitted previous generations, helping them understand that bad things can happen when self-interested people are not kept in check. It might also help some adults see our current situation with greater clarity.

—*Peter Cook, High School Teacher, Melbourne Australia*

Bischke serves up a cautionary tale both entertaining and dire—a cast of characters we recognize, and a message we ignore at our peril.

—*Alan Kesselheim, author of LET THEM PADDLE: COMING OF AGE ON THE WATER and ten other books*

This is a great allegory—I can really see the political stereotypes and how they parallel our society. The characters are universally western, not just American. We all know people like the fish in FISH TANK. I really liked that the book did not leave you hopeless, that there is good that will last. I read the book very quickly because I could not put it down! I would love my friends to read it and think the book would be a good book club book.

—*Gwen Laurie, former book store owner from Canada, age 78*

FISH TANK is a real eye opener! It depicts today's current social and environmental issues in a simplified way eliminating the confusing political and economic jargon which clouds the urgency of these concerns. It truly is a book for all ages because the future of our planet depends on everyone, not just a single generation.

—*Brittney Iverson, Marine Biologist*

I liked [FISH TANK] ALOT. One of the things I saw was the school culture that exists both at the middle school and the high school—the bully behavior—the trust issues—the respect that is given and missing. It was all there. And on another level, I could see the whole creation, God care, expectation, loss and recovery. It would make a great book club read!

—*Nancy Jordheim, Asst. Superintendent, Fargo ND Public Schools*

I think that [FISH TANK] was a great read. The storyline was great and the conflict was interesting and made you think about what the creatures could've [done]....For me the moral/message of the book was not to be greedy, to be aware of your surroundings. Greediness can never lead to happiness and if you're self centered it affects the people around you. To me, the book said that you need to listen to people. Being a know-it-all is never the way to go. Sometimes you're not always right.

—*Annie, student, age 13*

FISH TANK [is] a great read for all ages. It has many different layers that appeal to people of all reading levels, from the enchanting characters and plot to the deeper messages that leave you thinking. I was really able to relate the issues and characters in FISH TANK to issues and people that I deal with in my life. FISH TANK leaves you thinking about the role you play in our society and challenging yourself do better. It is a must read for all ages!

—*Tessa, student, age 14*

FISH TANK demands discussion. As I finished it I wanted to explore the connections and ideas more with someone. Given the concerns brought up in the book, I want to know how it will go for us humans? I am trying to see my place in it all—who am I? What am I doing in *my* world? How am I contributing to the problem or solutions? Do I need to change? I need to ponder the book's ending. Is there hope? Does anyone have any control?

—*Joan Exley, Community Literacy Coordinator, Province of BC*

An important story for our times. Let he who doesn't live in a glass aquarium cast the first stone!

—*Otto Pohl, entrepreneur and international journalist*

Not only is FISH TANK a page turner, it is an important wake-up call as we head towards catastrophe with our heads in the sand. Even sea-creatures have conflicts of interest, and in FISH TANK we see a story about how those that stood to make short-term gains endangered all life—surely this is the most important story of our modern society. By telling it as an allegory, and encouraging readers to see the parallels with humanity, Bischke's book could have a profound impact.

—*Dr. Raina Plowright, DVM and PhD Ecologist*

A fun, poignant exploration of human nature! [FISH TANK] reaches beyond the story of climate change and invites readers to look at the human dynamics that drive so many of the challenges faced by society.

— *Kate Burnaby Wright, Ecologist*

FISH TANK is an honest portrayal of the social dynamics that prevent us from confronting the problem of climate change. The events in FISH TANK demonstrate that our instinct to survive as individuals is much stronger than our instinct to survive as a species. The story challenges readers to rise above these base instincts and make the choice to face the problem together.

—*Natalie Meyer, Sustainability Director, City of Bozeman Montana*

[FISH TANK is] a great and important story—one that I hope will resonate with all who read it...It is a good way to talk about climate change and show how just one degree increase in temperature at a time can go unnoticed and have disastrous results. We are on our own to solve the world's environmental problems and we must not listen to nay-sayers who will only realize our plight when the sky comes falling down.

—*Tom Vandel, Owner, Les Overhead Advertising*

Although found in the fiction section, FISH TANK is truly a non-fiction story of our times with the [xxx] playing the part of the one percent. We can't be as foolish or complacent as the fishes. We can't be in denial like the fishes. Just as the "Occupy" movement has shouted its intolerance for corporate greed and corruption, it's time we do the same when it comes to climate. We need a revelation. FISH TANK forces you to realize just that.

—*Kelly Matheson, Program Manager, WITNESS, NYC*

I see glimpses of oil executives, or even commercial fishermen who are the biggest nay-sayers on depleting fish stocks even as it is harder and harder for them to catch their limit. People are quite shortsighted about climate change, huh? ... Also, Celia thinks the animals would not be so altruistic to not eventually eat the [xxx] when times got tough. I hope that doesn't happen in our world, but have you seen Mad Max?

—*Chris Slater, 7ᵗʰ grade English Teacher, and Celia, student, age 14*

An entertaining and enlightening tale, FISH TANK is especially pertinent in this age of global climate change. FISH TANK offers an insightful commentary on the way politics, policies, and our social structures combine to create the world in which we live. The reader finds himself wondering, "Is this the world we want to live in, to leave for our children? Can't we do better than this?" FISH TANK is a must read for anyone who cares about the future health of our planet...hopefully that's everyone!

—*Susie and Dennis Iverson, Education Specialist & HP Manager*

All throughout I interpreted the book to be about oil consumption and global warming. I think it would be a nice tool around Earth Day to get students thinking about these issues....I think the book's message is many-fold: moral, ethical, practical....[O]ne message of the book is certainly hope and the beauty of human ingenuity.

—*Susan Buhlman, Court Stenographer*

Reading FISH TANK I was repeatedly reminded of how we wrestle satisfying both personal and community goals; and how the details of human nature influence—for good or bad—complex issues like climate change.

—*Chris Mehl, City Commissioner, City of Bozeman Montana*

FISH TANK is exactly the type of book that I love to read and discuss. On one level, it is an enchanting story that draws the reader in...I can read it purely for entertainment value. But, there is also a deeper side...that captures the reader's attention and challenges them to think about their own role in contributing to the health and well-being of this planet that we all call our home.

— *Jody Ouradnik, Education Curriculum Content Designer*

[FISH TANK lays] out the dynamics of making decisions in the face of uncertainty and how power plays and denial can make the decisions so much harder. And there was a real emotional impact...For me it worked well both as an allegory and a story.

—*Kathy Brewer, Hewlett-Packard Environmental Engineer*

[FISH TANK is] a good story with a message—don't believe everything you are told and think for yourself! We are all in this boat, tank, universe together!

— *Dr. Janet Lindsley, Professor of Biochemistry, University of Utah & Stuart Vandel, Federal Reserve Bank examiner*

I loved FISH TANK...The message is at once hopeful while realizing its impending tragedy. It is regretful that everything must be so polarized....Perhaps the children of the 21st century will usher in a renewed sense of collaboration between environmentalists and industry.

—*Hattie Baker, Climate Change and Sustainability Consultant*

By peer pressure, misleading scientific data, fear, and our own stubborn nature to change, [FISH TANK] clearly shows why most people choose not to believe we have a real problem on our hands.

—*Bob Eichenberger, Business Manager, BOZEMAN DAILY CHRONICLE*

FISH TANK is so much more than a fable. It is a call to action to everyone who loves life and feels compassion in their hearts. It is a call to action to the privileged and powerful to act on the good within.... It is a call to action to the unions, to the workers, to the masses, who together can stand up to the corruption of the powerful. It is a call to action to the experts and our climate leaders to tell it straight and spread the solutions far and wide. It is a call to action to everyone, not to bury our heads in the sand and ignore what is right in front of our eyes while hoping for that Hollywood ending. It is a reminder to governments not to abuse the trust in which we have placed the well-being of this generation and the next. And it is a reminder, that when inspired and with timely action and a bit of personal sacrifice, we all can make a difference and change our fate, but only if we beat the tipping points. Scott Bischke opens floodgates of feeling for humanity and other species in this important book.

—*Julia Olson, mother and Executive Director, Our Children's Trust*

Fables have been part of human history since we began sharing stories around a campfire. The modern world, with instant communication and based on facts, offers little room for creative storytelling, especially ones that have a moral or lesson attached to them. FISH TANK is a throwback to the times of Aesop with a very modern and imminently relevant message. Children and adults alike will understand the predicament of the denizens of the aquarium and the parallel to humanity as we power ourselves into the 21st century. Take it as a great story, but know that it is real. If FISH TANK gets 10 people to adjust their life style it will have made a difference.

—Conrad Anker, elite mountaineer and author of
THE LOST EXPLORER: *FINDING MALLORY ON MOUNT EVEREST*

Frank and sometimes brutally honest, this is a tale of oppression of the group by the few who benefit without consequence.

—Dr. Robert Gresswell, USGS Fisheries Ecologist

This story of life in the aquarium is eerily similar to contemporary events outside the tank. FISH TANK is a good read, but more than that, it is a story about the forces of greed against the power of determination and collaboration.

—Dr. Cathy Whitlock, Director of the Montana Institute on
Ecosystems, Montana State University

In FISH TANK, the author represents planet Earth as a fish tank, and humanity as a bunch of talking fish of different species, interests and motivations engulfed in a very peculiar situation. What results is a clever and fascinating fable that provides an insightful mirror on the folly of current human attitudes concerning climate change and global degradation. Some people like graphs and data, the IPCC reports are written for them. But others connect better with concepts, imagery and storytelling, and for them FISH TANK should be compelling. It's hard not to contemplate if the human species is reaching some similar decision points, and a happy face outcome is not guaranteed.

—Dr. Steven W. Running, Nobel Laureate as a member of the
Intergovernmental Panel on Climate Change, Department of
Ecosystem and Conservation Sciences, University of Montana

Fish Tank

A Fable
for Our Times

by

Scott Bischke

* A MountainWorks Press Book *

Other books by Scott Bischke
(see www.scottbischke.com for more info)

TRUMPELSTILTSKIN – **A Fairy Tale** (MountainWorks Press 2016)

GOOD CAMEL, GOOD LIFE – **Finding Enlightenment One Drop of Sweat at a Time** (MountainWorks Press 2010)

CROSSING DIVIDES – **A Couples' Story of Cancer, Hope, and Hiking Montana's Continental Divide**
(American Cancer Society 2002)

TWO WHEELS AROUND NEW ZEALAND – **A Bicycle Journey on Friendly Roads** (Pruett Pub. hardback 1992; Ecopress paperback 1996)

FISH TANK
A Fable for Our Times

Copyright © 2012 by Scott Bischke

ISBN 978-0-9825947-1-1

LCCN 2011904318

Publisher—MountainWorks Press

An imprint of MountainWorks, Incorporated

Front material quote from: Orwell, George. _ANIMAL FARM_. New York: The New American Library, 15th printing, 1963.

FISH TANK is available in paperback, or Kindle and other eBook formats, with or without a discussion guide (the guide can also be downloaded for free at the author's website). Find Scott and his books at the website listed above, and on Amazon, Goodreads, and Facebook.

FOR THE CHILDREN

FOR THE FISH

FOR TOMORROW

Creatures of the aquarium

Ally	seahorse
Altair	seahorse
Big Moe	crab (big claw)
Dolly	damselfish
Dusty	flounder
Flecky	clownfish
Gabe	angelfish
Hammy	parrotfish
Hansom	goatfish
Jessie	turtle
Push	puffer fish
Roop	crab
Sanger	squirrelfish
Sarin	crab
Tommy	tang
Zuriela	angelfish

*It was soon noticed that when there was work to be done
the cat could never be found....
But she always made such excellent excuses,
and purred so affectionately, that it
was impossible not to believe
her good intentions.*

Chapter 1

PROFESSOR BROWN COULD HEAR Augustus banging around down below and wondered what he was doing. For the hundredth time the good professor shuddered at the thought of leaving his precious work in the hands of a full-fledged bumbler, an imbecile of the first order.

The professor stood at the top of the stairs to listen. More banging, this time sharp and metallic. He cringed.

Professor Brown buttoned his tattered sweater, then grabbed the railing and started stiffly down the long set of stairs to the aquarium. He told himself once again that he *had* to go to Australia; that this was surely his last shot at a sabbatical. Even this one seemed absurd. He'd been out of active research for

15 years and these days held only a cursory appointment at the university.

But Professor Brown had gotten lucky. For over four decades he had concentrated on a little studied, oft-forgotten, endangered seahorse measuring only an inch in length. And now a new oil discovery threatened one of three known populations of "his" seahorse. The deposit lay beneath the Indian Ocean floor right under the seahorses' home reef. Within a month of the oil discovery an ocean research institute in Western Australia had offered him a year-long sabbatical—paid, with a fully outfitted lab and a research assistant.

How could he possibly turn that down?

As he reached the bottom of the steps Professor Brown saw just how: Augustus, all square head and greasy overalls, was beating a rusty valve with a ball-peen hammer. The crack of metal-on-metal resounded through the room.

"What on Earth are you doing?" the professor asked.

"Tryin' to loosen the valve to let the fresh seawater into the fish tank, like youse showed me," responded Augustus, an accent from the old country coming through.

"It's an aquarium, Augustus, *not* a fish tank—how many times do I have to tell you?!" Professor Brown pulled off his glasses, then rubbed his mustache, a habit past students recognized as meaning he was annoyed.

"And look here, Augustus, all you do is lift this catch and then the valve opens easily, just like I showed you yesterday—remember? You don't have to bang on it! Besides it's supposed to be open all the time. Why did you close it anyway? Did you pay *any* attention during our training sessions?!"

"Oh yea, profess'r, sorry," Augustus said, stepping backwards and stumbling over a pipe wrench lying on the floor. "I remember all that, I do. I really do. Don't youse worry none, I'll 'member it all. See look, look—I filled the binny to feed all them fish for three or four days, jus' like ya showed me. See there?"

The professor did not look at the food bin. Instead he stared at Augustus in consternation. How can I trust this man? he thought. I have no choice, he realized once again. No one else had answered his ad for a caretaker; there were just not many people on this remote section of coast. So no one else was available, at least not at the price he was able to pay. He was stuck with Augustus, who said he could only come down to check on things twice a week owing to his job at the mill.

"Just go get the car, OK?" said the professor, turning away and putting his glasses back on. "You've got to get me over to the Eugene airport."

Augustus dropped the hammer on the floor, muttering something the professor couldn't make out, and started up the stairs. Professor Brown turned to follow, but then paused. One more look around, he thought. It'll be a year until I see this place again.

The aquarium had been his life's work, started 50 years earlier when he had taught inland at the university town. In those days he had only lived part time at the beach house. Still he had carried out all of his lab-based seahorse research here. The professor would proudly tell anyone who'd listen that he had authored over a hundred peer-reviewed publications based on work done in the basement aquarium at his beach house.

The beach house was an odd place on a remote section of the Oregon coast. It sat right at the end of a long, narrow basalt inlet, like nothing they'd allow you to construct today. Professor Brown had built the house over a cave of sorts, twenty feet down, then run two 50-foot pipes to link the base of the aquarium to the ocean. One pipe channeled sea water into the aquarium and hence brought his living lab to life. With each ocean wave the aquarium received a fresh surge of new water. The surges made the aquarium gently pulsate, giving the sense that the aquarium itself was a living, breathing being. A sump pump in the aquarium floor, screened at the inlet so that no creature could enter or exit that way, carried water back out to the ocean via the second pipe. A second sump, also screened, protected the room outside the aquarium.

The aquarium itself, as big as a Hummer, was a masterful work of thick, smoothly cut glass and caulking built into the corner of the cave. Two sides of the aquarium were relatively normal and boxy. The cave wall made up the third and fourth sides. One of the places the rock and glass came together was relatively smooth and the seal could be made fast and strong. The other seal, however, held the glass to a very rough section of cave wall; the roughness meant that the fourth corner of the aquarium required caulking every year or two to hold its seal.

The professor noted with satisfaction that his new caulking job from the previous day looked smooth and bright white.

The aquarium currently only housed two of the seahorses on which Professor Brown had made his career. At one point he had several dozen, but now the aquarium mostly consisted of an odd assortment of crustaceans, coral, and fish, all remnants from the time when he'd tried to make it as much like the seahorses' warm water environs as possible.

The professor brought in sun through a tube in the ceiling. Heating coils allowed him to gently heat the cool Oregon coastal waters to match the warmer waters where the seahorses lived.

While Professor Brown usually fed the creatures of the aquarium by hand—he always thought it best to spend time seeing how his creatures were doing— he was quite proud of the feeder he'd built for those times when he went away. It looked a bit like an inverted funnel with a hopper on top for fish food storage and a narrow tube that dropped from there into the water. The end of the tube allowed food to slowly fall into the aquarium for the fish to eat. Just above the tube, mounted on the side of the aquarium, was a valve that could be turned to adjust how much food was dispensed each day.

For a moment now Professor Brown did glance at the food hopper and indeed, as Augustus had said, it was full. The professor had designed the food hopper with enough volume to supply the aquarium for a week, the longest he'd ever been gone at a conference or on vacation. With Augustus hired to come in twice a week for the next year, the safety factor seemed sufficient.

Satisfied that the food was in place, the professor knelt and pushed his nose against the glass. Even at 78 he retained the child's joy of gazing into the aquarium, never tiring of wondering what the fish were thinking, wondering if they knew they were not in the outside world but instead in an environment of his creation.

At that moment the two seahorses hovered opposite him across the glass. "I will see you in a year," Professor Brown said as much to himself as to the seahorses. "In the meantime I'll see what I can do for your brethren down south." The seahorses seemed to stare right back at him, gill plates rhythmically opening and closing, almost as if they were in conversation.

"Professor, we gotta go." Augustus's call from upstairs brought Professor Brown out of his reflections. "I forgot ta gas up the car like youse told me so we need to hurry or ya might be late."

Professor Brown sighed. He stood and walked to the stairway, then shifted his cane to his left hand and reached for the light switch. Suddenly the professor had the odd sensation of being watched and a chill ran down his spine. He took one last look back. At that moment the aquarium's lone turtle—a young Ridley he'd relatively newly acquired— floated at the top of the water column. It was a creature that would eventually outgrow the aquarium, the professor knew, but he had agreed to take it as for the moment it was small and unobtrusive.

As the professor watched, the young turtle lifted its head above the surface and looked at him.

Professor Brown drew up short—for one sublimely strange moment his eyes locked with those of the turtle and he was certain he could sense a look of worry in the turtle's gaze.

No, couldn't be, you crazy old man, he thought. The professor turned, switched out the light, and began the long climb up the stairs.

Chapter 2

THE TURTLE'S LOOK, INTERESTINGLY enough, *had* been one of concern. For the young turtle, whose name was Jessie, knew that with Professor Brown gone and no one to watch over them, the crabs—Sarin, Roop, and Big Moe—could be trouble.

It all started soon enough, just five days after Professor Brown departed. The crabs called the creatures together. They convened near the corner where the aquarium glass mated with the rough wall of the cave. The cave wall had a large ledge there, a stage of sorts. Sarin, the crab ringleader, stepped into the center of the ledge flanked by compatriots Roop and Big Moe.

"Listen up," Sarin said. The creatures shushed. They were variously circled around the crabs: the shrimp stood at attention; Tommy Tang, Sanger the squirrelfish, Hammy the parrotfish, Push the puffer, and Hansom the yellow goatfish floated quietly. Small schools of wrasses, gobies, and grunts flitted back and forth, finding it hard to stay still. Dusty, a curmudgeonly old flounder, lifted a sleepy eye from beneath the sand while Flecky the clownfish peered out from the protection of some anemone stalks. Jessie the turtle looked down from above the rest.

"It's been five days since Professor Brown left and we have not been fed," said Sarin the crab. "The professor would have been here every day. But you heard what he said before he left—he is gone for a year and has left us to the devices of that idiot Augustus."

"Yes, Augustus," Roop, the others crab, chimed in with disdain. "Aren't we lucky to have brilliant Augustus? Perhaps we should call him 'AgainstUs' instead."

The other creatures chuckled.

"Yes agreed, AgainstUs is more appropriate. But this is *not* a laughing matter," Sarin continued, silencing the chuckles. "AgainstUs has been coming for three weeks and done nothing for us, nothing, even during the time when Professor Brown was right upstairs! AgainstUs simply looks down from above with that big stupid grin of his, watching us, treating us like children."

"That's right," said Hammy the parrotfish. "AgainstUs couldn't even open the inlet pipe without messing up. What use is he anyway?"

"Well of some use, I should surely think," replied Hansom, a goatfish so respected for his intellectual bearing that within the aquarium he was known as "Doc". Hansom continued, rubbing his whiskers in contemplation, "Without Augustus we won't get fed. Assuming he does return—don't forget he's getting paid—I would call that being of some use, wouldn't you?"

A murmur went through the crowd.

"*Get fed*, what do you mean *get fed*?!" It was Push the puffer now, his face bloated and turning crimson. "Even if AgainstUs shows up he's only going to be here twice a week!"

Tommy the blue and gold tang swished his tail lightly to move into the circle. "I dare say, Push, you are the last one of us who should be worrying about getting his feedings."

More laughter. Push glared at Tommy.

Jessie the turtle chimed in from above, somewhat timidly as she was just getting to know the others, "Remember when the professor told Augustus that the food hopper would last for a full week? It's only been five days. Maybe Augustus will be back in a day or two."

"How can we be sure about that?" asked Sanger the squirrelfish, dismissing the turtle with a scoff.

"I bet AgainstUs is dead," chimed in Flecky the clownfish dramatically, "and that means we are all going to die!" Flecky darted into the safety of the anemone as the others looked among themselves.

Then the seahorses, Altair and Ally, spoke. They were small and spoke quietly so the others had to quiet and lean in to hear. Altair and Ally had the odd habit of completing each other's sentences. "No, Augustus is not dead," started Altair. "The last time the Professor went away...."

"...his students messed up at the beginning, too," Ally continued. "Augustus will do just fine..."

"...and it will all work out this time, just like it always has." Altair finished their thought with a satisfied sideways glance at Ally.

Sarin the crab had been watching this chatter go back and forth, eye stalks alternating between speakers. "You are all innocent imbeciles," Sarin said with disgust.

"Imbeciles," repeated Roop, rolling his eye stalks to show his agreement and irritation.

Sarin drew up and pointed into the crowd with one claw. "Here's what you need to understand. We can never—I said *never*—count on AgainstUs! AgainstUs doesn't care a lick about any of us. We can only rely on ourselves."

Chapter 3

AUGUSTUS, IT WAS TRUE, had no interest in the aquarium. None. All he wanted was the money. Still Jessie the turtle had been right about why Augustus missed his first stop in to see the aquarium three or four days after he had dropped Professor Brown at the airport.

"Food binny will last a bless'd week," Augustus had rationalized while sitting on the couch at home. "Fish tank will do jus' fine 'til the weekend. Then I'll go down."

At the end of the first week Augustus *did* make it back to the aquarium. When he filled the food hopper he noticed that it wasn't completely empty. He knelt and tapped on the glass. A tang, a small turtle, and a dozen wrasses hovered at his eye level, staring out at him.

"Youse louts don't need as much food as the professor thinks, does ya?" Augustus snarled. "Tell ya what, if I made a few of ya inta appetizers, you'd need even less!"

Augustus straightened up with a small growl. The tang and the turtle rose to near where the feeding tube entered the aquarium, appearing intent on his every action. Augustus surveyed the food hopper, looking it up one side and down the other. Slowly he smiled a toothy grin, an idea apparently fixing itself in his dim mind.

"All I gotta do here," he said aloud to himself, "is make the food binny bigger and then I won't ever need to come back. Ol' Auggie will jus' collect the money 'til the professor comes back next year!"

The idea stuck in his mind like a fly on dirty fly paper. For days Augustus schemed as he worked at the mill, collecting materials and tools when others weren't looking. By the end of the week he was back at the aquarium with a plastic 55-gallon drum, a long rope, a roll of duct tape, and a bunch of 2x4s.

Using the 2x4s, Augustus built a pedestal for the 55-gallon drum directly over the existing food hopper. He cut one end of the drum completely off, then cut a smaller hole out of the drum's other end. The smaller hole just fit over the original food hopper. Next Augustus did some fancy work with the roll of duct tape to make sure the 55-gallon drum and the food hopper mated nicely, with no chance for food to leak out. Standing on a rickety chair, he then drove hooks into the wall and ceiling. Augustus tied one rope from the hooks to the pedestal, and another down to a fastener inside the drum, helping stabilize the entire affair. Finally, he shook his contraption hard and noted with satisfaction that it seemed solid, unmovable.

As Augustus worked the creatures of the aquarium emerged as one to watch. There were three crabs, a school of gobies, a parrot fish, a squirrelfish, and more, all lined up against the glass.

Next Augustus grabbed a number of huge sacks of fish food, ripped off the tops, and poured them into the 55-gallon drum. Soon the drum was full.

Work complete, Augustus wiped his brow as he stepped back to survey his handiwork. "Very nice if'n I do say so me'self. You be a smart man, Mr. Auggie," he said, now bending down to look at his smug reflection in the aquarium glass. "The professor 'll never know ya didn't come to the fish tank, and you'll be a richer man 'cuz of yer smarts!"

As Augustus basked in self-praise, he became aware of a movement beyond his reflection, beyond the glass. At first he saw the flicking tail of the yellow goatfish, then a blue and gold tang, then a school of pearl wrasses. As he refocused his eyes into the tank he realized that all of the creatures of the aquarium were just across the glass, all of them staring at him. What on Earth is going on here, their expressions seemed to say.

Augustus shook his head, suddenly uncomfortable. "Youse all there in the fish tank," he growled, pointing, "youse can go stuff yerself for all I care! I'm done here."

With that Augustus turned away and started up the stairs, scattered fish food bags still littering the floor.

Chapter 4

THE WEEK AFTER AUGUSTUS constructed his 55-gallon drum feeder passed quietly. Each day the creatures of the aquarium ate their fill. Sarin and the crabs had quieted for the most part and, except for Push the puffer complaining about not being hand fed each day, the aquarium operated pretty much as normal.

It was Hansom—the distinguished looking and highly intellectual goatfish—that first sounded the alarm. At that moment Hansom, Jessie the turtle, and Tommy Tang were hovering near the surface looking up to the food hopper.

"I dare say," said Hansom, thoughtfully stroking his whiskers, "Augustus's new hopper doesn't look anywhere close to being big enough to last out the year."

"How can you say that, Doc?" asked Tommy Tang. "It looks like endless food to me."

Jessie paddled up until her head poked above the surface. Upon returning to the other two she said, "I...I guess I agree with Tommy." Jessie spoke reluctantly as she had begun to idolize Doc Hansom and his scientific ways. But still she continued, "I don't think we could ever eat all that food. The drum looks full almost to the rim."

THREE MORE WEEKS PASSED. Everyone ate their fill and life in the aquarium remained uneventful. Hansom the goatfish, however, continued to study the food bin. And he continued to quietly share his concerns about the food running out with Tommy Tang and Jesse the turtle, the latter of whom the good doctor found increasingly tagging around with him.

While none of the three said much, word soon got around to the creatures of the aquarium about Hansom's concerns. Rumors quickly began to circulate. One rumor had it that the creatures of the aquarium would have to begin rationing food; another rumor said that the food tube had clogged. Flecky the clownfish declared that Augustus had purposely filled the food drum with rat poison.

Knowing that he was smarter than anyone in the aquarium, many of the creatures began to come to

Hansom the goatfish to ask his opinion. Hansom decided to do some more rigorous calculations. He estimated the size of the old food hopper and compared it with the addition of Augustus's 55-gallon drum. With those estimates, and knowing that Professor Brown said the old food hopper would last a week, he could readily calculate how long the feeding drum Augustus made would last them.

"Not nearly enough fish food for all of us for a year," was Hansom's firm conclusion. "My calculations show that at the rate we are eating now we have enough food for around eight months."

IT HAD NOW BEEN over eight *weeks* since Augustus built his extended food hopper. By this point Hansom the goatfish had explained his calculations to anyone who would listen, sometimes many times over. He'd improved his calculations by adding an estimate of the food in the feeding tube. But he had also subtracted a bit to account for a slight slant in the drum, a slant that meant not all the food would make it into the aquarium. Hansom now believed they had just seven months of fish food supply.

Given all Hansom's talk and effort, it did not take long before Tommy Tang and Jessie the turtle began to believe that he was right. Soon, so did a number of others.

But it wasn't just Hansom's logic and persistence that caused the other creatures to stand up and take notice. You see Augustus had not returned, not once. As such Hansom's calculations began to be discussed more and more. What if, the creatures of the aquarium wondered, Augustus really does not come back until the end of the year when Professor Brown returns? Is it possible there really won't be any more food this year?!

Talk around the aquarium began to get louder. Most of the talk focused on the amount of food in the 55-gallon drum, but the rumor mill continued to churn. Strange ideas got bantered about, though none stranger than Flecky the clownfish stating flatly that Augustus planned to come back and throw a stick of dynamite into the aquarium.

AROUND THIS TIME THE three crabs called a second meeting at the big ledge near the corner of the aquarium. Most of the creatures attended, except for Hansom the goatfish who said he didn't have time to interrupt his studies.

Once again Sarin the crab stepped onto the center of the ledge, flanked by Roop and Big Moe. "Listen up," Sarin demanded. The creatures came to attention. "I've heard the rumors about a food shortage—I know you've all heard them, too. Well I am here to tell you those rumors are ridiculous!"

"Ridiculous!" echoed Roop.

"We have endless food," Sarin continued. "We will never run out of food. Those that are saying otherwise are simply alarmists!"

"I used to think that, too, Sarin," said Tommy Tang from the crowd. "But Doc Hansom calculated it out and if Augustus doesn't come back with more food then…"

"Quiet you buffoon!" It was Push the puffer. "Let Sarin talk."

"We will *never* run out of food!" Sarin repeated the same words just louder, causing the gobies to shudder in fear and retreat behind a rock. "That old goatfish only wants to inflate his own self importance! Just stop and think—have any of you had to eat any less in the last month? Anyone losing weight?"

The creatures of the aquarium looked among themselves, then broke into a chaotic chorus of voices. "Not me," said one of the shrimp. "Nor me!" said another and then another.

"Have you been hungry, dear?" asked Gabe the angelfish to his spouse. Zuriela shook her head. "Nor I," said Gabe.

The wrasses schooled about with the gobies, questioning each other, and not one of them could recall being hungry.

"No, actually I haven't lost any weight," said Dolly the damselfish, surveying her reflection in the aquarium glass, "but I surely wish I would. Just a little anyway."

The commotion lasted a full minute until finally Big Moe stepped forward on the ledge. Big Moe tended to be quiet as compared to Sarin and Roop, but unlike the other two crabs Big Moe had a feature that demanded attention: a single gigantic claw almost as big as the rest of his body. Big Moe slammed the claw on the ledge, and yelled, "Silence everyone!"

The crowd exchanged nervous glances as they quieted. Then Push the puffer spoke for them, "Of course you're right Sarin. We've all been eating as much as ever. Our lives haven't been impacted one bit."

"So right," said Roop the crab, Hammy the parrotfish, and Flecky the clownfish as one.

"Exactly!" shouted Sarin, now standing on hind legs. The looks of fear had subsided from the faces of the creatures. "We have a right to be happy, and live well my friends. That's why I'm telling you all to eat to your heart's content!"

Chapter 5

IT WOULD BE ANOTHER month before the animals assembled again. In the interim Tommy Tang, Jessie the turtle, and Altair and Ally the seahorses met many times to discuss the pending shortage of food. Others were invited to join them but no one else chose to attend. After a dozen meetings the small group decided to voluntarily eat ten percent less at each meal.

"The four of us are choosing to eat less," Tommy, Jessie, Altair, and Ally told anyone who would listen. "If everyone else would just do the same, the aquarium's food crisis could be averted."

Roop the crab was there when Tommy revealed the food rationing plan to the shrimp. After Tommy swam away Roop said emphatically, "Those four are speaking nonsense. They must be some kind of stargazers!"

The shrimp gasped as one. To call a member of the aquarium community a *stargazer* was the lowest blow one could deal them. Every one of the creatures recognized a stargazer as a sneaky creature that hides in the sand and kills with venomous spines—a danger to them all.

"Nonsense!" said Push the puffer. He had waited until after Jessie left from talking to the wrasses, then swept in. "Don't believe anything those four say!"

In the weeks since the great food drum debate began, Push had seen the sway the crabs held over the creatures. Though he was bigger than most of the others, Push's insecurity led him to throw his lot in with the crabs—regardless what they might say—so he could have more clout and respect in the aquarium.

The wrasses looked at Push with uncertainty until he said, "You know of course that those four are just a bunch of useless stargazers."

The wrasses expression turned to horror.

Across the aquarium Hammy the parrotfish hovered among a school of gobies. Hammy had long idolized Push the Puffer. So when Push moved to back the crabs, Hammy immediately mimicked Push's words. "Careful if Altair and Ally come by," he told the gobies. "They've been speaking nonsense. We think they might be working with the stargazers."

The gobies all nodded solemnly.

Later, when Sarin the crab spoke to a couple of grunts, a sizeable group of others gathered around. "*Eat less*," Sarin said incredulously. "What nonsense! It sounds like our friends have been hanging out with one too many stargazers."

INTERESTINGLY, EVEN HANSOM THE goatfish did not give Tommy Tang, Jessie the turtle, and Altair and Ally the seahorses much support. Hansom's negative reasoning, however, differed greatly from the rest of the creatures.

When the four of them came to ask for Hansom's help in defending their plan to voluntarily eat less, Hansom responded, "Your goals are noble, but your sacrifice will not save the aquarium. In that I agree with the others."

"What?" said Altair. "But you're the one...."

"...who started this whole thing," finished Ally.

"We believed in you!" said Tommy, gill plates flashing.

"Yes, Doc, we did," said Jessie dejectedly. As young Jessie aspired to the sciences like Doc Hansom, she took his negative words especially hard.

"No, wait a minute. You don't understand," Hansom responded. "It is *worse* than we thought.

Even if we could get everyone to eat *half* their normal amount, we would only delay the inevitable. My newest calculations show that *even then* we would all still starve to death in ten months."

Tommy, Jessie, and the two seahorses groaned in anguish. Hansom said nothing more, instead just shrugged as if to say, "Sorry, but the numbers don't lie."

WITHIN A SHORT TIME of announcing their food rationing plan Tommy, Jessie, Altair, and Ally had been labeled *stargazers* by a great many of the creatures in the aquarium. But still they pushed forward, buoyed by Hansom's newest calculations, certain that they were right, certain the fate of the aquarium rested on the creatures listening to them.

Having fared so poorly in their one-on-one interactions with the aquarium creatures, the four decided to call their own group meeting to see if they might better get their message across en masse. The crabs—Sarin, Roop, and Big Moe—advised everyone not to go and listen to those "stargazers", but as there's not much new to do when you live in an aquarium, most everyone went anyway.

While the creatures gathered around—wrasses, gobies, grunts, and more—Tommy Tang swam up onto the big ledge in the corner of the aquarium. Jessie, Altair, Ally, and Hansom joined him, hovering nearby. The crabs stood off to the side, each looking healthy and seemingly larger than a month earlier. They stood in front of the anemone, flanked by Sanger the squirrelfish, Push the puffer, Hammy the parrotfish. The shrimp, whom stargazers frighten greatly, attended but huddled closely together. Dusty the old flounder was also there, but settled into the muddy bottom, saying he didn't want to be bothered by it all.

"My friends," Tommy began, "we have asked you here to discuss a very serious matter. It has now been over 12 weeks since Professor Brown left, ten weeks since Augustus built the big food drum. I think we can all now be pretty sure that Augustus is not coming back to feed us again, at least not until near the end of the year so he can take down the food drum before the professor returns."

A murmur of general agreement ran through the crowd, interrupted by Sarin yelling, "And good riddance. AgainstUs is good for nothing—we don't need him!"

"Be that as it may," Tommy continued, "we need to start considering what we are going to do about food. It should be clear to all that we *will* run out of food before the year is out. Doc Hansom says...."

Here Push the puffer interrupted Tommy by shouting, "You lie!" An instant later Hammy the parrotfish yelled, "Yes, you lie!"

Instantly Flecky popped out of the anemone and screamed, "Stargazer! Stargazer! Stargazer!" Flecky darted back into hiding, but his brief appearance was enough to start many in the crowd chanting, "Stargazer! Stargazer! Stargazer!"

Sarin looked on with an amused smile.

Tommy, clearly ruffled, turned to his compatriots and shrugged. Hansom the goatfish drew himself up and finned to the center of the ledge. Such respect did the distinguished goatfish garner that the creatures immediately quieted, leaving only Push and Hammy still chanting. Embarrassed, they stopped.

Hansom stroked his whiskers, then spoke slowly. "We are in a very precarious position, my friends, one that we cannot simply wish away. We are in grave—I daresay imminent—danger of running out of food before Professor Brown returns."

Every creature was transfixed on Hansom as he continued, a hint of contempt creeping into his usually flat tone. "Sarin encouraged you all to eat without restraint. You have done so now for a month, putting us in even graver risk than we were before."

The creatures looked from Hansom to Sarin. Sarin scowled as Hansom continued, "A while back I calculated that Augustus left us enough food for just eight of the twelve months Professor Brown will be gone. Now my calculations show that we will run out by the end of month six if we continue to eat as we have been doing. That's only three more months."

Dolly the damselfish gasped; the wrasses swooned; one of the gobies, clearly pregnant, said, "What will happen to my babies?"

"And know this," Hansom continued, speaking over the commotion, "when the food runs out—and assuming Augustus doesn't come back it surely will—we will all starve to death."

Sarin raised up on hind legs, claws extended, and shouted, "The good doctor has gone batty on us! Wacko! These are lies, I tell you, we have endless food!"

"If you don't believe me," Hansom said, ignoring Sarin and continuing to address the crowd, "why not just look up at the food drum for yourselves? When Augustus left us it was full, now it looks to be almost half empty. Yet it has only been three months since Professor Brown departed. That food has to last us nine more months. You don't need my fancy math to see that we are in big trouble."

Groans sounded from the creatures as they all looked up through the water column at the food drum.

That's when Sanger the squirrelfish, nudged by Roop the crab, finned forward into the conversation. "Nonsense!" he cried out.

Sanger held ill repute among the creatures, but also grudging respect as he was the only one of them who could even come close to keeping up with Doc Hansom intellectually. "The good doctor has once again stretched the bounds of science."

"Quack," came a muttered call from down on the aquarium floor. It was Dusty the flounder, emerging from the bottom to show that he had indeed been listening and was visibly upset with Sanger. But when Dusty caught sight of Big Moe's evil stare, he slid quietly back under the sand.

Sanger pressed on, his big eyes looking ever so much like spectacles. "Are you not aware, my friends, that water bends light? The 'half empty' drum Hansom describes is nothing of the sort."

A confused hum ran through the crowd. "What are you talking about?" asked Gabe the angelfish.

Sanger had by this point nudged his way up onto the ledge. "The light is bent when it goes from air into water and that distorts the view," he continued. "I have myself calculated the angles of incidence and refraction and can assure you that what you are looking at is a mirage. In fact the drum is still 90 percent full. Forget what you see, there is indeed endless food!"

The creatures of the aquarium looked among themselves, still confused. Then Roop the crab began to chant, "Endless food! Endless food!"

Quickly Push, then Hammy, and then Flecky— the latter newly emerging from the anemone—took up the chant: "ENDLESS FOOD!"

In a moment the shrimp joined in and then the grunts, and then most of the other creatures, including the worried goby mother, chanted, "ENDLESS FOOD!"

Later, as the chanting subsided, most of the creatures began to disband, smiles on their faces. Hansom the goatfish looked at the departing crowd with a mixture of pity and disdain. He turned to his compatriots and rolled his eyes, but said nothing.

Chapter 6

FOR A MONTH HANSOM the goatfish, with Jessie the turtle often at his side in support, worked to convince the creatures of the aquarium that Sanger the squirrelfish was mistaken. Hansom talked of wave propagation in different mediums and refractive indices and showed them complicated equations and charts of bending beams of light. Scientifically, it all proved beyond any doubt that Sanger had been dead wrong about the level of food in the bin being a mirage.

For many, the good doctor's explanations were not enough. First of all the gobies, wrasses, grunts, and others did not understand his explanations. Second, the creatures were regularly bombarded by far simpler counterclaims from Sanger, backed loudly by the crabs and Push, Hammy, and Flecky.

In the end it was Jessie who finally hit upon irrefutable evidence that Sanger's mirage explanation was a hoax. Each day the young turtle spent hours floating on the surface of the aquarium. Each day she looked at level of food in the drum. Day-by-day Jessie could not detect change, but week-by-week she was certain she could see that the dark line marking the top of the remaining food had moved.

As the fourth month wore to an end, Jessie noticed something especially troubling: the dark line indicating the top of the food supply was now nearly as close to the top of the original hopper as it was to the middle line on the drum. And for the first time she noticed something else that she reported to Hansom and Tommy Tang.

"The food level is dropping fast," said Jessie. "We've all known that for some time. We are down to at most a fourth of the big drum."

"Yes," said Hansom, stroking his whiskers but not looking up. "Most troubling, most troubling indeed."

Tommy added sadly, "I fear that we had all better start hoping against hope that Augustus returns to feed us soon...."

"But wait," Jessie interrupted, her voice infused with youthful excitement. "There's something else I noticed today. I don't know if it's important, but it seems like it could be..."

"Yes, my young friend," said Hansom, "what is it?"

"I noticed that the amount of food left in the drum looks the same when compared to the entire drum, regardless of if I'm down here with you or up at the surface. The overall size of the drum is different, but the percent of the drum that's full remains the same."

Jessie now had Hansom's complete attention. "Of course, that's it!" Hansom exclaimed, his eyes suddenly animated.

It is?" said Tommy and Jessie as one.

Hansom darted forward and swam a celebratory circle around the pair, unable to withhold his exuberance. "Yes, my dear friends," he said when he stopped. "Jessie has solved the problem of Sanger!"

"I have?" said Jessie.

"You have! How could I be so stupid? Every day you have reported back on your vision from the surface and every day I have listened and set it aside. But the ratio, my girl, that is the key!" Here Hansom pulled himself up to his full stature.

"Sanger made calculations that I have clearly refuted. But sadly no one is smart enough to understand the math so they chose to believe what serves them best. 'Still 90 percent full even after four months'—what poppycock!"

Tommy and Jessie exchanged confused glances. "Sorry Doc," Tommy said, "we're still not following you."

"Sanger's calculations—wrong and harebrained that they be—describe refraction, in other words what happens when light passes between air and water. None of the creatures but me has the brains to understand the math, *but they don't need to!*"

"They don't?" this time it was Jessie again. She felt proud of her discovery, but still uncertain what it meant.

"No, my dear," Hansom continued, "you showed that we can remove refraction from the picture. All we need to do is get our fellow creatures to swim to the surface and look through the air as you did! Then Sanger's argument falls apart and they will have indisputable evidence that the food crisis is real!"

IT TOOK A WEEK for Tommy, Jessie, Altair, and Ally to fully disseminate Hansom's revelation to the creatures of the aquarium. At first they did not believe it, but eventually Gabe and Zuriela, the angelfish couple, decided to swim to the top and have a look for themselves. They lay on their sides, poked their eyes into the air, and saw that it was just as Jessie had told Hansom.

"It's frightening," said Gabe to a gathering of wrasses and gobies. "So little food left. Perhaps a fourth of the drum."

"Surely no more," Zuriela added. "I'd even say less than that!"

The report from the angelfish caused many of the other creatures to swim to the surface to have a look for themselves. Even Dusty the flounder rose up from the bottom. None disputed the claim that the drum was three fourths empty.

And Sanger the squirrelfish had no rebuttal.

Soon the wrasses, gobies, grunts, and more believed they were in peril. Only the shrimp, who could not get to the surface, held out that Sanger might still be right. That all ended when Jessie the turtle piggybacked one of the shrimp up through the water column to have a look for itself.

The shrimp's report back to its cohorts left the crabs plus their cronies Push, Hammy, Flecky, and Sanger the only deniers of the aquarium food crisis. But with such overwhelming evidence, and now with near unanimous agreement to the problem, the food shortage deniers were forced to abandon their claims of endless food.

IN THE COMING DAYS, Sarin and Roop huddled to consider what to do next. They knew that to retain any influence and control—and surely that is what motivated them—that for the moment they had to move in concert with the will of the creatures. They would stay vigilante, the two crabs decided, to find a place where they could take command and mold the creatures' will again.

In truth, it can now be told, the crabs knew that the food in the drum had been dropping since almost the beginning. For unlike most of the creatures they were able to crawl up the cave wall and exit the aquarium whenever they wanted, something the others always envied.

"It's not that great," the crabs always told the other creatures. "There's no food out there and no way to escape the lab so we just sit on the wall and do nothing."

The crabs' statement had been true enough until Augustus built his extended food drum. What the crabs did not tell the others is that they had made a startling discovery: the rope Augustus used to anchor the drum was hooked directly to the wall they rested on. Within days of it being installed, the crabs realized they could shimmy down the rope directly into the food drum.

Nightly for over three months, while the creatures of the aquarium slept, the crabs had been eating their way through the year's food supply like kings.

NOW THAT THE CREATURES of the aquarium all accepted the food crisis as fact, they gathered to debate what should be done. They talked about instituting a food rationing program such as that long ago proposed by Tommy Tang, Jessie the turtle, and Altair and Ally the seahorses. While the debate was at times lively, most of the creatures could see no way around the need for rationing. Only Dolly the chunky damselfish and the goby mother-to-be spoke against cutting their food rations.

As the creatures seemed to be reaching consensus, Gabe the angelfish posed another possible solution: "What if Augustus comes back? If he wanted, Augustus could just fill the food drum up again and we would all be fine."

"That's right," said his spouse Zuriela. "If Augustus comes back to take care of us, then all of this worry will have been for nothing."

Though reserved of late, this talk was more than Sarin could stand. "You are talking pure idiocy!" the crab yelled out.

"Idiocy!" echoed Roop, then Push, and then Hammy.

"AgainstUs doesn't care about any of you. Not one lick," said Sarin. "He only wants to take the money from Professor Brown and give us nothing in return. The less we see of AgainstUs, the better off we are!"

The seahorses, uncharacteristically, came forward to challenge Sarin. They looked even smaller than usual next to the big crab, who seemed to be gaining girth. "Would we be right, then..." started Ally.

"...to assume you would agree to rationing?" finished Altair.

"No," answered Sarin. "And do you know why? Because you are forgetting someone."

"Who..." "...would that be?" asked Ally and Altair.

"Professor Brown," answered Sarin emphatically. "We do not need rationing, we simply need to believe in Professor Brown."

"But he's not here," said Tommy Tang, joining the seahorses.

"Of course he is here," Sarin returned. "Just look out at the lab. Professor Brown created this all and he won't just let us die. Surely wherever he is the professor knows that AgainstUs can't be trusted. Professor Brown will return and feed us."

A rumbling of dissent ran through the crowd. So even though Roop, Big Moe, Push, and Hammy nodded in agreement with Sarin's comments, it wasn't enough. None of the other creatures seemed inclined to Sarin's position. Soon the grunts, wrasses, gobies (except the mother-to-be), and all the rest swam into place behind Tommy, Jessie, and the seahorses. Only the shrimp, who seemed at least open to Sarin's thoughts, stayed put. Sanger the squirrelfish and Flecky the clownfish were nowhere around.

With the creatures thus separated, Dusty the flounder flipped his tail in the sand, throwing a dust cloud up to displace Sarin. This time when Big Moe glared at him, Dusty glared right back.

Hansom the goatfish came forward into the spot vacated by Sarin and the rationing discussion began anew. Proven right about the food shortage, Doc Hansom had returned to even greater favor among the creatures of the aquarium.

"I support rationing, in principle," Hansom said, "but a ten percent reduction as was once proposed won't be nearly enough. Instead, I have calculated that 50 percent reductions *by everyone, every single day* will be required. We should actually cut back more than that, but I fear many of us would die just from the rationing itself."

Several of the creatures gasped.

"I am sorry, but I have worse news," Hansom continued. "Time has passed since I worked up my last model. But I have reworked my calculations. Previously it had appeared that we could make it to ten months if we had started on 50 percent rations.

But with all the food we have eaten that is no longer true. Even if starting today we only eat half as much as we used to, we will only be able to stay alive through the seventh month of Professor Brown's absence."

"Seven months, Doc!" cried out Gabe the angelfish. "Are you saying that even with rationing we will *still* starve to death?!"

"Again, I am sorry," Hansom continued, speaking more to the assembled group than just to Gabe. "But as our friend the angelfish has surmised, we will not be out of the woods even with drastic food rationing."

The creatures' faces had turned ashen.

"My friends," Hansom continued, "let me be clear. There is not enough food to sustain us for the year. Rationing will not solve our problem, but we still must do it to buy ourselves time to come up with an actual solution."

Hansom finned backwards to let his thoughts settle. As little discussion ensued, Tommy Tang finned forward to say, "This is a major commitment, my friends. I recommend that we all think about it for a while and then come back to vote."

The creatures disbanded slowly, the wrasses behind their rock, the shrimp into recess in the cave wall, others variously scattered about. Hammy the parrotfish followed Push the puffer over to the anemone while the three crabs shuffled off into a distant corner of the aquarium.

When Tommy Tang reconvened the creatures, it was Sanger the squirrelfish, now returned, who immediately finned forward, ignoring Tommy but pointing his question directly at Hansom. "My dear goatfish colleague, the others have filled me in and I must say that in this rare instance I am now inclined to agree with you. We must do something. But I have a quibble. The food simply falls in the tank. Have you considered how we might cut the amount by 50 percent?"

The creatures looked to Hansom, who rubbed his whiskers thoughtfully. "The solution is quite easy, actually," he said. "We simply need to turn the control valve on the food hopper. The food dispensed each day will slow, and we will buy ourselves some time to come to a better solution."

"Yes," responded Sanger, "I had come to the same conclusion. And I suspect we both have the same idea how to turn the valve. Big Moe, with that huge claw of his, should be able to grab the valve and close it half way."

The creatures turned to Big Moe, who was off to the side next to Sarin and Roop. Big Moe said nothing, but did raise his big claw to show his willingness.

Some of the creatures expected Sarin or Roop to argue. Instead they nodded their heads slightly, indicating tacit agreement with the plan. In truth they had no choice. They had only recently realized that even their nighttime binges in the food bin would end when the drum went empty. Restricting the flow of food into the aquarium to the other creatures was the best bet they had for self preservation.

After Hansom said, "Indeed, yes, I had been thinking of Big Moe as well," Tommy opened the floor to all. Once again little discussion ensued—the creatures seemed resigned to their plight. In the end they voted without joy to accept Hansom's 50 percent food rationing plan.

NONE OF THE CREATURES of the aquarium slept well that night. Some worried about feeding their children. Some worried about not having enough to eat for themselves. Some worried about what would happen to them when the food ran out.

But some—three to be exact—spent little time worrying. Instead, the reason they slept little was that they were too busy up in the food drum eating.

Chapter 7

FOOD RATIONING PROVED HARD on the creatures of the aquarium, though the first week started gently enough. When stomachs first growled lots of nervous laughter could be heard. Most of the creatures found themselves looking more often than normal to see if any food was dropping into the aquarium. Dolly the damselfish's friends kidded her that she might finally get rid of that extra weight she was always talking about. But for the most part life went on as usual.

By two weeks after the rationing started life had turned far less pleasant. Dusty the flounder suffered headaches. Zuriela the angelfish became sick. Gabe started giving her most of his own food in hopes of bringing Zuriela back to health. The wrasses regularly withdrew behind a large rock; they'd hover there lethargically for hours swaying rhythmically with the surge of the ocean water coming in through the inlet pipe.

By two weeks later the negative impacts of the 50 percent rations had become even more apparent. The creatures looked visibly weakened. Now almost everyone, not just the wrasses, struggled to hold their position in the water column. They moved little except to catch the limited fish food as it sprinkled down to them.

Surprisingly few tussles occurred over the falling food. Most of the creatures stuck to their agreement to eat only their allotment. Only Push the puffer and Hammy the parrotfish regularly stole more than their fair share. But they argued that as they were bigger than the others, they deserved more.

"Plus," Push said, "and I don't mean to be indelicate here, but some of you eat our ordure. Thus if we get more, you get more."

"Let's face it," added Hammy, wanting to add to Push's words, "that *is* the way the world works."

The rest of the creatures of the aquarium had little energy to put up a fight with the two bullies. Hunger occupied their every waking moment. Almost all were thin, in some cases hollow, shells of their former shelves.

Along with Push and Hammy, only the crabs seemed no worse for the rationing wear. Though their power and influence had diminished since the food rationing decision, Sarin, Roop, and Big Moe still moved about the aquarium pretty much as always. To the others the crabs' physical stature did not appear to have diminished; if anything they looked to be growing.

One day Tommy Tang pressed the crabs to explain why they appeared to be doing so well. Roop responded first: "Unlike anyone else we have hard shelled bodies that don't shrink. You just can't see our suffering."

"But rest assured," added Sarin, "we are miserable, just like all of you."

SINCE THE ONSET OF the rationing program Tommy Tang, Jessie the turtle, and the two seahorses Altair and Ally had continued to regularly convene the creatures of the aquarium. The creatures had a pressing need to consider their options ahead. Daily they sent Jessie to the surface to monitor the amount of food left in the drum. Although the rationing had stemmed the precipitous drop, it still appeared to the creatures that the food in the drum was disappearing faster than they could account for.

On the day that the emaciated goby mother lost her brood, Tommy called the creatures of the aquarium together once again, the sense of urgency palpable. "We are at the beginning of our sixth month since Professor Brown departed," Tommy Tang said. "Conditions are dire."

"Tell us something we don't know," groaned Dusty the flounder. No one laughed. Dusty could barely lift his head from the sand. His headaches had become incessant and he looked as thin as a rug.

Jessie, who had grown into her position as the data provider, continued for Tommy, "Our monitoring shows that we are down to ten percent of the food drum remaining. Long ago Doc Hansom told us that even with rationing we would only make it to the end of the seventh month, and he appears to be right."

Gabe the angelfish, eyes withdrawn, let out a sigh.

"But we must not give in, my friends!" Tommy jumped in again. "We must continue to fight! We have options and we still have time."

Tommy's excited demeanor then turned solemn. "But here is an option we will not give in to, a path we cannot follow." He paused for drama befitting what he was about to say. "In recent days our friends the gobies and wrasses have become fearful for their lives. Some of you, apparently, are talking about eating fish again!"

A collective gasp rose up from those assembled. Zuriela the angelfish cried out, "No that can't be!"

Neighbors looked at neighbors, wide-eyed, fearful, and wondering.

"Zuriela is right," Tommy continued, "that *cannot* be. On joining the aquarium community we all agreed to put aside our carnivorous ways to live off Professor Brown's fish food. *Every one of us agreed!* If we start to eat each other, what kind of life would that be?"

"No life at all," said Dusty, this time more emphatically. "But then this is no life either. We must do something or we'll all be dead soon!"

"We'll all be dead! Oh my God, we'll all be dead!" It was Flecky the clownfish, emerging from the edge of his anemone hiding spot. "And you know why we'll be dead—because of AgainstUs!"

The creatures turned to look to Flecky, but Tommy Tang quickly finned forward to take back center stage. "That may well be true," he said, "but it's also irrelevant. We need to do something now if we are to survive. It's long been apparent that we can't count on Augustus coming back before the end of the year."

Tommy paused and drew himself up, fins flaring. "These are desperate times, my friends, and in desperate times we need to open our minds to new ideas. That's why I've asked Doc Hansom to address us today. He has a radical new idea that we just might want to consider. Doc...."

Hansom the goatfish finned forward. But before he could speak, Sanger the squirrelfish asked skeptically, "And what, pray tell, is the good doctor going to suggest this time?"

"There is only one way that we can save ourselves," Hansom said, ignoring Sanger's corrosive tone. His voice did not rise or fall like Tommy's; he simply spoke in a matter-of-fact manner. "We have to begin to grow our own food—our own algae stocks—if we are to survive."

A collective shudder ran through the crowd. There was a moment of silence, and then in another moment creatures started yelling out chaotically.

"We don't know how to grow our own food!" cried the shrimp in unison. "We're not farmers!"

"Who will be responsible?" yelled Gabe the angelfish.

"But I only eat protein!" howled Push the puffer.

"Me, too!" shouted Dusty the flounder, and then more quietly, "or at least I prefer it."

"I hate algae," cried Dolly the damselfish. "It's bad for my color!"

"Will there be enough food for my fry?" asked one of the wrasses.

"But wait, Professor Brown will surely come back to save us!" Roop the crab cried out.

"Professor Brown! Professor Brown!" yelled Flecky the clownfish.

Jessie the turtle paddled forward and waved to the crowd to be quiet. And then the two small seahorses, Altair and Ally, came forward. It was not lost on the creatures of the aquarium that their entire existence owed to Professor Brown's love of the seahorses. Thus the creatures quieted to listen with rapt attention to the soft-spoken seahorses.

"We must do this," said Altair. "We must begin to grow our own food. Otherwise..."

"...we will all die," Ally continued. "We can't rely on Professor Brown. Yes, he cares about us but..."

"...he also left us to our own devices." Altair again took up their thoughts. "He would expect us to do what we have to do until he gets back."

The seahorses slipped back behind Tommy Tang while the creatures began to discuss among themselves what they just heard. Tommy decided to let them converse for a few moments, but suddenly Sarin stepped forward to seize the moment, realizing this might be a chance for the crabs to regain control of the aquarium.

"I agree with our two little friends," Sarin started. Looks of surprise came over more than a few faces in the crowd. "We *must* become self reliant and take on the responsibility of growing our own food so that we can take care of ourselves. True some of us will need to forgo the nice taste of the fish food but...."

Though located far apart, a simultaneous groan went up from Push the puffer and Dusty the flounder.

Sarin gave them each a dirty look, then spoke more loudly, "...but we can learn and adjust and be better than we are today!" Sarin raised two claws overhead and then, as if claiming Hansom's idea, shouted, "And by growing our food we can have *more and better food* than we have ever had before!"

The creatures looked uncertainly among themselves, surprised at Sarin's gush of exuberance. Doc Hansom, Tommy Tang, and Jessie the turtle exchanged glances, uncertain of Sarin's motives, but as the crab seemed to be pushing in the direction they advocated, they stayed silent.

Finally, Dolly the damselfish broke through the commotion asking, "More food?"

"Yes *lots* more food!" responded Roop for Sarin.

"Better food?" said Gabe the angelfish.

"Yes," said Roop, "better food than you've ever eaten!"

Flecky the clownfish suddenly emerged from the anemone and began to chant, "More and better. More And Better! MORE AND BETTER!"

By the third chant one of the shrimp joined Flecky, and then another, and then another. Soon the entire shrimp brigade was shouting "MORE AND BETTER!" in chorus. The wrasses soon joined in, then the gobies, then more and more of the creatures as the crescendo built. When Push the puffer and Dusty the flounder remained silent, at least not arguing, all seemed in accord.

Sarin nodded to the clownfish, then turned to the chanting crowd. "This will be good for you," the crab said, "you will see."

Chapter 8

DURING THE FIRST WEEK after their decision to farm algae the creatures moved in fits and starts. Not surprisingly, Push the puffer and Dusty the flounder continued to protest the change, not being willing to give up their rich fish food. The other creatures could be happy as vegetarians, so for them the change to algae was no big deal. But not so Push and Dusty, who suddenly formed a somewhat awkward alliance.

"I don't eat algae," Push groused.

"Nor I," added Dusty. "Yuck! It's unfair!"

Sarin the crab confronted their concerns head on, asking just what they thought they got from the fish food anyway.

Push paused, uncertain. Finally he said, "Well I guess I don't know. I never thought about it."

Dusty shrugged, showing he clearly didn't know either.

"Protein," Sarin said. "You get protein. And guess what, if we grow Spirulina algae, you can get all the protein you need."

Push and Dusty exchanged glances. Both looked dubious. But Sarin had been prepared and asked Hansom the goatfish to sit in on the discussion. In fact, that's where the crab had learned about the protein. At first the goatfish had demurred, but Sarin had been insistent and he had relented.

"It's true, is it not good doctor, what I said about Spirulina?" asked Sarin.

"Yes," said Hansom, looking up from rock he was scrutinizing, "that was mostly correct. But Spirulina is actually a photosynthetic cyanobacterium, not a eukaryotic algae...."

Sarin quickly interrupted, "Yes, yes, I'm sure that all might be important, but about the protein?"

Hansom glared at Sarin, looking like he might leave, but then turned to the crab's desired path: "Spirulina *is* quite high in protein. It can serve as a source of many amino acids, vitamins A, B12, C and E, a whole range of minerals...."

"Got it, Doc, got it," this time Sanger the squirrelfish interrupted. "And beta-carotene, and more. That's all great, but mostly what's important here is that Push and Dusty could survive on Spirulina. Would you not agree?"

Thus pressed Hansom paused, reflective. When he looked up he said, "Well in principle I suppose it is surely possible. But perhaps not opti...."

"Perfect, we got it Doc." It was Roop the crab who cut in this time. He tried to pull the discussion to a close saying, "So you see, Push and Dusty, you will not only survive but thrive on the new algae diet. Isn't that great?"

Sanger, along with Hammy the parrotfish who hovered nearby, nodded their heads in enthusiastic agreement with Roop's words.

"Ok, maybe it will work," said a dejected Push, looking to Dusty.

Dusty appeared less convinced, squinting at Roop in consternation. Then he popped up out of the sand with a new idea, saying, "But wait a minute, there is still a bit of the fish food left up in the drum. Why not let Push and me eat that, at least until it's gone?"

Push's eyes changed from downcast to suddenly hopeful.

Now true, the crabs agreed with the conclusion that growing algae was the only way the creatures of the aquarium, including themselves, could survive. But they had no intention of letting anyone but themselves eat the remaining fish food. Thus Sarin had prepared for this question, earlier working the disgruntled Sanger toward a solution to the posed problem that suited the crabs' desired outcome.

"Because, you simpleton," Sanger said, responding to Dusty before anyone else could, "we need nitrogen from the fish food to fertilize the tank. Without it we won't be able to grow enough food for us all."

"Doc is that true?" asked Dusty dubiously.

"Well surely the algae need nitrogen, yes," said Hansom. "But how much? To know that we need to know how much nitrogen we have in the water already, how much nitrogen is in the fish food, how much the algae take up as they grow, how much algae we plan to grow, the temperature of the water, how much space…"

"Doc, say it so we can understand, OK?" Dusty asked.

"Sorry, yes, my friend," Hansom said, coming out of thought. "It is a big question, a big question indeed."

"So there you have it," Roop said, jumping in with an air of obvious conclusion. "We must save the remaining fish food for fertilizer. Let's get about our business now. Planting needs to begin soon."

Hansom looked puzzled at the sudden wrap up of the discussion. But as the others started to move off, apparently accepting Roop's words, the goatfish said nothing and instead turned back to his studies.

THE DECISION ON WHAT kind of algae the creatures of the aquarium would grow proved to be a no brainer. Professor Brown had once inoculated the aquarium with Spirulina and though it had not flourished, some remained. It grew best on the aquarium glass. A second variety—a bubble algae— also existed in small patches in the aquarium. It grew best on the aquarium floor.

So two forms of algae would be grown.

The crabs, it turned out, had a special affinity for bubble algae. None of the other creatures could stand it.

IT WAS NOW A month after the decision to begin farming. Jessie the turtle watched the busy activity in the aquarium below with amazement. Each day the creatures made progress. Spirulina coated a portion of one of the aquarium's glass walls. Two plots of bubble algae took up space on the aquarium floor.

As Jessie watched, she saw Tommy Tang calling the creatures of the aquarium together. Jessie paddled down excitedly to join them.

Tommy appeared gleeful. "My friends," he began, "we are into the seventh month since

Professor Brown's departure. We would not have made it to this point without our shared sacrifice, without rationing our food. But even with that, it is the month that good Doc Hansom predicted we would die. And as our monitoring showed today, we are indeed down to less than five percent of the food drum remaining."

Many of the assembled creatures groaned, some hissed, but the atmosphere was one of celebration, not despondence.

"Not going to happen!" shouted one of the grunts joyously. Many of the creatures laughed and clapped.

"Today is the day," Tommy continued as the crowd quieted, "that we have all been waiting for!"

"Yes it is!" cried Gabe the angelfish.

"We did it!" yelled the wrasses and gobies.

"Indeed we did do it," said Tommy, enjoying the moment as much as any of them. "For today is the day we agreed that we could begin to eat the fruits of our labor!"

"Let's eat!" shouted Dolly the damselfish.

The creatures moved to bolt, but Tommy's voice stopped them short: "Wait, please! Do not forget, we have only just begun this wonderful effort. We cannot eat all of the algae in a single setting! Be conservative, my friends. Eat slowly, enjoy, but eat just a little so that we will have more tomorrow!"

Tommy was lucky to hold them that long and when one shrimp bolted, and then another, the flood gates opened and the creatures were gone. All but the three crabs raced off to indulge in the Spirulina they had so carefully tended for a month.

THE CREATURES OF THE aquarium largely decimated the Spirulina crop that first day of eating. So devastated was the Spirulina supply that some of them even tried to eat the bubble algae, but all found it revolting.

Invigorated by their binge, the creatures quickly set about rebuilding their new found food source. They cultivated new areas of glass for Spirulina, and though they suffered for a time more while the crop grew back, all now believed they could overcome hunger for the remainder of the year.

BY THE START OF the eighth month after Professor Brown's departure, life had returned to some semblance of normal in the aquarium. All of the creatures were putting back on weight at prodigious rates. Neat, well kempt crops of algae grew on the aquarium walls and floors.

For the moment, all seemed well with the world.

Chapter 9

FOR WEEKS THE CREATURES lived a charmed and happy life. Their happiness contrasted greatly with the dire outlook that had been their collective reality not that long ago. Day-by-day the algae grew and grew, creating a general sense of euphoria. The great food crisis had been averted!

The creatures no longer sulked in dark corners or hovered languidly in the water column. Instead they flitted about the aquarium with energy, some even joyfully riding the surge as fresh ocean water poured in through the inlet pipe with each wave train. The goby mother-to-be was pregnant once more.

That's not to say that all was perfect. Push the puffer and Dusty the flounder complained daily about their new diet. Push still seemed to eat as much as ever, even as he complained, but Dusty ate only grudgingly.

Whenever Dusty complained, Tommy Tang, Jessie the turtle, and the others would urge him to just be patient. "Professor Brown will be back in four months and we will once again be eating fish food," they said. "Hang in there—you just have to make it until then!"

Only the crabs joined Push and Dusty in being unhappy with their new diet. True, Sarin, Roop, and Big Moe counted their lucky stars that they were the only ones in the aquarium to like bubble algae. Still, they liked fish food better, of that there could be no doubt. But what really worried the crabs was that since they'd discovered the path down into the food drum, they'd eaten like gluttons every night. Now they faced the prospect of having their food source limited to several small patches of bubble algae, and that caused them no small sense of panic.

How can we continue to grow? the crabs wondered.

Initially the crabs focused on the last of the fish food in the drum. Each night they ate without reserve. Each day Sarin sent Sanger the squirrelfish out to remind the others that they must not eat the fish food filtering down from above. Instead they were to let it settle and fertilize the algae. Whenever one of the creatures said that the drum seemed to be emptying far faster than the food fell, Sanger assured them his calculations showed that all was in order.

WITHIN TWO WEEKS THE food in the drum was gone. The creatures of the aquarium noted the milestone sadly, but no longer did they fixate on the food drum during every waking moment. They stopped sending a lookout each day to monitor the drum. Instead, the creatures tended to their Spirulina.

With the fish food gone, the crabs turned their attention to their bubble algae crops. It took only a few days for them to realize that the patches that existed barely served them. Each night they felt uncomfortable, and heretofore unknown, hunger pains.

The crabs did not like being hungry.

HUNGER IS A GREAT motivator, causing Sarin and Roop to scheme unendingly about what they might do. (Big Moe said little; he was mostly happy to just listen to the other two crabs talk.) Sarin and Roop quickly realized they needed more production, but they had a big problem: the only way they knew to produce more bubble algae was to plant more. And since bubble algae did not grow on the glass like

Spirulina, to plant more they needed to appropriate more of the aquarium floor.

That's where the problem came in. Much of the aquarium was covered in swaying anemone, coral, inedible sea weed, and other surfaces not conducive to growing bubble algae. Other parts of the aquarium floor would work, but they were already being used as home ground by Dusty the flounder and the big group of shrimp.

So space in the aquarium was limited, but Sarin and Roop developed a plan.

Sarin called the creatures of the aquarium together one morning to make an announcement. All the creatures showed up, buzzing with excitement as it had been some time since they had gathered.

"With the food drum empty," Sarin started solemnly, "we are forced to face facts. We no longer have enough nitrogen to fertilize your Spirulina crops."

The mood dampened considerably and the creatures tuned in more closely to hear what Sarin was saying.

"The Spirulina," Sarin continued, "I am sorry to say, will soon crash, as determined by Sanger."

As the creatures turned to look at Sanger the squirrelfish, their attention was suddenly pulled away by the prattling voice of Flecky the clownfish, "It's gonna crash and WE WILL ALL DIE!"

Sanger welcomed the interruption to gather his thoughts as he and Sarin had never talked about what would happen to the Spirulina when the food bin emptied. But by the time Flecky disappeared back into the anemone and the creatures turned to him, Sanger had made his decision.

"Yes it's true," he said. Sarin and Roop exchanged satisfied glances; their gamble had paid off. They had long known that Sanger wanted little more than to be recognized as the intellectual equal of Hansom the goatfish. By calling Sanger forth as the expert they had massaged the squirrelfish's ego in just the right place.

"When the food bin empties and there is no more nitrogen supply," Sanger said, "the Spirulina will die." Sanger paused, uncertain where the story would go next, but Sarin quickly filled the void.

"But we have a way to solve the problem," Sarin said. Sanger shook his head in agreement, though he had no idea what Sarin was planning to say. "If we increase bubble algae production we will increase the amount of nitrogen in the water and that, in turn, will save the Spirulina crop."

"You see the bubble algae *give off* nitrogen that the Spirulina can use," added Roop.

"That's great," said Push the puffer.

"You've saved us!" beamed Hammy the parrotfish.

"Now wait a minute," said Tommy Tang, finning forward to interrupt the conversation. "Doc Hansom, is any of this true?"

Several of the wrasses parted so that Hansom the goatfish, who had been quietly listening, could be seen. "As I once told you," Hansom said, "yes the Spirulina need nitrogen. But as to the rest I deal in data and facts, not speculation. I *can* tell you that the growth rate of both of our algae crops will increase with increasing light and temperature. Those are facts and anything else I say would be mere speculation without more data."

A pleased look came to Sanger's face as he jumped forth and confidently stated, "We must increase bubble algae production to produce nitrogen to save the Spirulina crop to save ourselves. Those, my friends, are the facts."

A mumbling passed though the crowd until Jessie the turtle spoke out, her voice showing considerably more confidence than when she'd first come to the aquarium, "And how do you propose to increase bubble algae production?"

"We will need to cultivate more of the floor of the aquarium," Roop said emphatically.

"Wait a minute," said Dusty the flounder. "The aquarium has very little open floor space left and much of it is where *I* live."

"There will still be plenty of space for you, Dusty," said Roop. Dusty, already upset with the Spirulina diet, did not look convinced. He looked, in fact, downright aggravated.

"And us," chimed in one of the shrimp, looking directly at Dusty. "What about us? You're not the only one that lives on the bottom." Several of the shrimp shook their heads in assent. "We need the food and we are perfectly willing to give up some space so that we will have more and better food."

"So *the crabs* will have more food," Dusty started to say, trying to point out who would first, and possibly only, gain benefit from the plan.

But Sarin spoke over him, drowning out Dusty's words. "Thank you for that vote of support, my shrimp friends. We will count on your help." Here Sarin gestured a claw to the assembled creatures of the aquarium, "We will count on *all* your help as we move forward from here."

THE CREATURES NOW MOSTLY in agreement to the plan, four new plots of bubble algae were soon under cultivation. The shrimp, so sure of Sarin and Roop's words, took over the planting and tending of the aquarium's entire bubble algae crop. Big Moe supervised the shrimps' work, but otherwise the crabs did nothing to aid in the effort.

The shrimp worked long hours, wearing themselves thin. Though visibly depleted compared to the past weeks of good times and plentiful food, the shrimp appeared happy. They loved working in concert for a plan on which they all agreed. The shrimp regularly defended the crabs' scheme to grow more bubble algae as not all of the other creatures felt so sure it made sense. Few of the shrimp could put into words why they agreed with the plan. In the end they stated their support by harkening back to an old mantra: "More food!" they would yell. "Better food!"

Dusty the flounder soon found himself newly crowded into a small section of the aquarium bottom. He grew more and more aggravated by the day. Tommy Tang's pleas that Dusty remain patient for Professor Brown's return did nothing to calm him.

Chapter 10

WITHIN A MONTH THE overall production of bubble algae topped that of Spirulina. The creatures of the aquarium continued to subsist successfully on the Spirulina; while all appeared generally healthy, none of them were growing.

The crabs proved the lone exception to this observation. Each day they spent the majority of their time eating through the plots of bubble algae. And they had just molted again, resulting in added weight and girth.

EVEN WITH THEIR PLAN being executed to perfection, the crabs were not satisfied. They huddled one night to consider how they could further improve their lot.

"We must grow if we are to control the aquarium," Roop said. "While we can get Push and Hammy to do our will, I worry that someday they might realize that they are bigger than us."

"Agreed," responded Sarin. "We *must* grow! And to do so we must find more food. We must fend for ourselves in any way we can."

Big Moe, so often quiet, said hopefully, "It won't be that long before Professor Brown returns to feed us."

"We can't wait for Professor Brown to bring us more food," said Sarin derisively. "Sure we can continue stringing the shrimp along with the promise that all will be better when the professor returns. But we are crabs, for goodness sakes. We must grow and we must grow now, not in 12 weeks!"

"You are so right my friend," said Roop.

The crabs' options, as they saw them, were limited. Though the crabs knew they could convince the shrimp to cultivate as many plots as they demanded, by this point essentially all surfaces conducive to bubble algae growth were already in production. The crabs talked about adding Spirulina to their diet but that idea died quickly—all three of them found the taste of Spirulina revolting. Next they discussed ripping out Spirulina and replanting the plots with bubble algae, but tests early on had shown that the two algae grew in entirely different environs so that idea didn't seem a realistic possibility, either.

The harder the crabs thought, the more they ran up against dead ends. Nothing seemed to make sense as a way to expand their food supply.

Finally Roop said, "I long for those good days after Augustus filled the food drum."

"Me, too," said Big Moe.

"Yes, those were the days," agreed Sarin.

THE NEXT DAY SARIN, Roop, and Big Moe decided to approach Hansom the goatfish in hopes he might help them with their dilemma. The goatfish, the crabs knew, could be of use to them but only if they asked the right questions.

"Greetings, good doctor," said Sarin when they met. "Roop, Big Moe, and I are trying to figure out how we can help all the creatures of the aquarium. We hope that we might ask your advice on how to grow more food."

"Hold on a minute," answered Hansom in an aggravated tone. For several moments he continued deeply concentrating on something in front of him. Eventually, head still down, he said, "What is it you want?"

"As you know the good of the aquarium creatures is always our central focus," Roop started.

Here the goatfish finally lifted his eyes, looking at Roop, then the other two, with an expression that seemed to say, "Hmmm." Hansom noticed that the crabs looked bigger than he last remembered. "Are the creatures asking for more food?" he asked. "I haven't heard that myself."

"Yes, yes," answered Roop, "every day they complain. Gabe and Zuriela feel they could still gain some weight, the wrasses are always hungry, the grunts grumble incessantly, and the goby mother is pregnant again." Of these statements only the story about the pregnant goby mother was true. But Roop thought the others to be small exaggerations—OK perhaps white lies—but surely, he reasoned, all the creatures would want more food if they could have it.

"A noble idea, then," said Hanson, accepting Roop's explanation.

Looking relieved, Roop continued, "So what we want to do is to increase the production of Spirulina to help the creatures better thrive through these last 12 weeks until Professor Brown returns."

"And the bubble algae?" asked Hansom somewhat skeptically. "I assume you want to increase production of bubble algae, as well?"

"If that was a side benefit of our discussions with you, that would be fine," Sarin jumped in. "But it is our concern for the other creatures that drives us."

Hansom rubbed his whiskers, seemingly unconvinced. But he said nothing, indicating to the crabs that they should continue.

"We have run up against many brick walls in our deliberations over what to do," continued Sarin, "and Sanger has been no help at all."

Big Moe gave Sarin a cross ways look as he knew the crabs had never asked Sanger for advice on this matter. Sarin scowled back, careful that Hansom did not see, and Big Moe knew to say nothing. For Sarin had judged correctly that because of the intellectual rivalry between the goatfish and the squirrelfish, this teensy additional white lie might help open Hansom up to address their questions.

Hansom smiled and drew himself up a bit under Sarin's subtle compliment. "I assume you have considered cultivation area?" the goatfish asked. The crabs nodded in concert. "And did you conclude that we have largely used up all productive surfaces?"

"We did," said Sarin and Roop in harmony.

"And did you consider incident light?" asked Hansom.

"No, we didn't. What do you mean, good doctor?" asked Roop.

"The algae need light to grow, so with more light we would improve productivity. It is one of the few knobs we might turn to increase our food output. But alas our light is controlled by the sun tube Professor Brown brought down from the ceiling. I don't see any way we can change our light source, or the other two knobs that might help."

"Other two knobs?" asked Sarin.

"Yes, I suspect that if we could increase the temperature in the aquarium we would induce the algae to grow more rapidly. Or if we could enrich the aquarium with nutrients—nitrogen, phosphorous, potassium, perhaps others—we might be able to stimulate more growth. But neither of these ideas is possible, either. First off, even if we could increase the temperature—which we can't— some of the fish would suffer, maybe even die. Second, we have no access to fertilizer, which is what the second idea really describes."

The two crabs looked disappointed. "We hadn't come up with any of those ideas," Roop said.

"Alas, they are nice concepts, good for theoretical discussion but ultimately impractical." The goatfish's tone indicated that he was concluding the discussion.

But after Hansom turned away, a final thought struck him. He turned back to the crabs, saying, "I daresay, I would suggest to you three that we all just hunker down for 12 more weeks. Life is relatively good right now. Let's enjoy what we have and look forward to the day when Professor Brown returns and we eat fish food again. Now if you will please allow me, I need to get back to my studies."

THE THREE CRABS GATHERED again that night. Roop had a big smile on his face, though neither Sarin nor Big Moe knew why.

"Why are you smiling?" Sarin asked.

"I have the answer!" Roop said.

"You do?" asked Big Moe, wide-eyed.

"I do," returned Roop. "Well actually, I suppose that the good doctor provided the answer to us, but I am the one who figured it out!"

"Figured what out?!" asked Sarin impatiently. "Fess up!"

Roop leaned in. "The doctor has twice now told us that if we increase the temperature of the tank, we can increase the growth rate of the algae. He dismissed the idea but...," and here Roop paused dramatically, "...we know something that he doesn't."

"We do?" asked Big Moe.

"Every night when we climbed up into the food drum we passed by something on the wall," Roop said with excitement. "Do you recall what it was?"

Big Moe looked befuddled but a light bulb suddenly went on for Sarin. "The thermostat!" Sarin said. "Every night we passed by the thermostat that controls the temperature in the aquarium."

Roop's smile grew big as he could see his plan gel in Sarin's mind. "No one else in the aquarium even knows the thermostat exists, it's hidden from view," said Sarin with glee. "If we turn the thermostat up to increase the temperature we can drive up the production of our food supply! Then we can continue to grow." Sarin paused momentarily before adding, "All we need to do is figure out how to turn the thermostat up."

"I've already figured that out," Roop said, happy to jump in and reveal the key part of his plan. "Big Moe will use that big claw of his to turn the thermostat, just like he did with the control valve on the food hopper."

Big Moe, who had been looking back and forth between them, brightened a bit as he finally understood the plan being formulated. But just as quickly his look turned dour. "What about what the doc said?" asked Big Moe. "If we turn up the temperature it might hurt some of the fishes."

"Collateral damage," said Sarin. "Nothing more. I tell you what, Big Moe, we'll turn it up slowly and the fish won't even notice."

"Look Big Moe," said Roop, joining Sarin in the argument, "in this world we must all look out for ourselves. And that means the three of us must always do what's best for crabs first."

"Crabs first!" echoed Sarin. "We need to do this so that we can continue to grow. Trust me, Big Moe, the others are only looking out for themselves. So are you with us?"

Big Moe had rarely spent much time thinking on his own. Instead he generally found it easier to just follow the lead of his two compatriots. He felt uneasy having a thought that did not match theirs.

For a moment Big Moe sat silent, eyes downcast, feeling his compatriots' glares. The moment dragged on, making Big Moe increasingly uncomfortable.

When at last he looked up, Big Moe stammered, "OK, I guess...." He hesitated again, but finally Big Moe waved his big claw weakly and then, trying to muster more conviction than he felt, said, "...crabs first it is."

Chapter 11

IN THE WEE HOURS of the next morning, while the creatures of the aquarium slept, Big Moe crawled unnoticed up the cave wall and out of the water. Using his gigantic claw like a wrench, the crab gently turned up the thermostat just a notch.

In the months ahead, Big Moe would repeat that process every night.

ZURIELA THE ANGELFISH WAS the first to comment on the changing fortunes of the Spirulina crop. It was a month after Big Moe had started his forays out of the aquarium under cover of darkness. Zuriela and Gabe were tending the crop, plus periodically stopping to eat.

"Is it just me," Zuriela said, "or does the Spirulina seem to be growing faster these days?"

"No it's not just you," said Gabe, looking up from his grazing. "I've been noticing it, too. Every morning we seem to have more to eat than the day before!"

The other creatures soon also noticed the increasing growth. A new sense of euphoria settled over the aquarium. The gobies and the wrasses and the grunts ate without reserve. Push the puffer, who had grudgingly taken to the Spirulina, seemed far less grumpy than usual. Hammy the parrotfish swam around with his cheeks constantly bulging. Jessie the turtle even caught Dusty the flounder smiling once.

While the shrimp seemed to be thriving, as well, they kept up their hard working ways on the bubble algae. We must produce more, seemed to be their mantra. And indeed, the bubble algae crop had almost doubled.

The crabs, likewise, looked bigger.

AROUND THE TIME ZURIELA made her observation, the seahorses noticed something, as well. They were hovering over the bottom, near the corner of the aquarium, when Tommy Tang swam up.

"Tommy," said Altair before Tommy could even greet them, "does it seem to you...."

"...to be any hotter these days?" Ally finished their question.

Tommy pulled up short. "Funny you should mention it. Yesterday Jessie told me she thought it seemed hotter on this end of the aquarium than usual. But it's always hotter here, isn't it, because the incoming ocean water enters from the other end."

"That might be true…," said Ally.

"…but I don't think it's ever this hot," finished Altair.

Tommy shrugged as if to say, "Who knows?" He swam on, but decided to look for Hansom the goatfish and see what he might have to say.

Tommy found Doc Hansom up along the crack between the aquarium glass and the cave wall, seemingly deep in thought.

When Tommy asked Hansom what he thought about his discussion with the seahorses, the goatfish's answer was short and to the point, "Doesn't matter what I think or how I feel. Just go look at the thermometer mounted on the aquarium glass. That will give you your answer."

Hansom went back to his inspections, leaving Tommy Tang to wonder why he had not thought of such a simple answer.

THREE MORE WEEKS WENT by. Algae production continued to sky rocket. But by now most of the creatures of the aquarium were talking about the heat, not about their bountiful food supply.

Tommy Tang called the creatures to a meeting near the thermometer to address the problem. The crabs were still making their way over from one of their algae patches when Tommy started.

"As you know," Tommy said, "many of us have been thinking that it's been getting hotter. And many of you thought we should talk about what we can do. So let's talk."

With the invitation thus made the creatures began to set out their concerns. The grunts and wrasses grumbled that they were having a hard time sleeping. Dusty the flounder complained of headaches again. Dolly had developed a disturbing sore on her side, much to the damselfish's consternation.

Initially, only the crabs demurred. "It's not hot in here," Sarin said acidly. "Nothing has changed. You're all imagining things." Roop, standing side-by-side with Sarin, nodded his agreement.

The crabs' feelings were well known by this point and Sarin's words came as no surprise.

Jessie the turtle, though a bit intimidated by Sarin and Roop, paddled forward and said quietly, "How can you say that? We all feel the heat."

Here others shouted their agreement.

"And what's more important," continued Jessie, emboldened by what she had to say next, "we have data! The thermometer on the side of the aquarium says it's getting hotter. We can all see it, plain as day. We are up two degrees since we started tracking three weeks back."

"Poppycock!" said Roop. "You can't believe that thermometer. Tell them Sanger."

Sanger the squirrelfish came forward, as requested. Of late the crabs had arranged for the shrimp to handle Sanger's cultivating duties in the algae patches, so he looked rested and strong.

"What Roop says is correct. That thermometer hasn't worked in years." Sanger paused, looking around for Hansom before continuing. Not seeing the goatfish, he proceeded confidently, "Actually, I daresay my own studies have found the instrument to be so imprecise that it is my professional opinion that the temperature is just as likely to be going down as to be going up!"

Jessie couldn't believe what she was hearing. Roop and Sarin had satisfied looks on their faces. Push the puffer swam over behind the crabs, followed quickly by Hammy the parrotfish.

Jessie looked to Tommy Tang, and then they both looked for Doc Hansom. But the good doctor was far across the aquarium, hovering near the corner of the glass and the cave wall.

"But it *is* real," Tommy said, wishing desperately he had Doc Hansom to back him. "We have watched the temperature rise with our own eyes. And we can all feel it."

More affirmations sounded from the crowd, though with less oomph than before Sanger spoke.

"It is *real*, is it Mr. Tang?" Roop's voice had a mocking tone. "What's *real*, it sounds to me, is that there are some *real* differences of opinion here."

"It's not real, NO WAY IS IT REAL!" It was Flecky the clownfish, emerging from and then disappearing back into a nearby anemone that he had taken up residence in for the meeting. Sarin spoke next, drawing everyone's attention away from Flecky. Thus no one saw when Big Moe, responding to silent urging by Roop, pushed a batch of Spirulina into the anemone.

"I tell you what I would suggest," said Sarin. "I think that we need a more careful study. Perhaps we could create a committee to look into these allegations—and let's be *crystal clear* that they are nothing more than allegations. Perhaps we could meet in a few months after compiling all of the information we have."

"Sounds smart," said Push the puffer.

"Brilliant!" echoed Hammy the parrotfish.

"But..." Tommy started to speak again but the crabs, Push, and Hammy had already turned to leave.

Shortly, the brigade of shrimp followed and then the rest of the creatures dispersed.

"THE MEETING WENT HORRIBLY, Doc," said Tommy Tang. He and Jessie had tracked down Hansom the goatfish several hours after the meeting at the thermometer.

"Where were you?" asked Jessie. "We needed your support. We needed your input so we could stand up to Sanger."

"Sanger is an imbecile," Hansom said dismissively. "And I am sorry for your troubles. But I fear that we may have a much bigger problem at hand."

"A bigger problem?" said Tommy.

"What could be a bigger problem, Doc?" asked Jessie. "Some of the creatures are already getting sick from the heat."

"Yes, I have heard that," said Hansom dispassionately. "But what I've discovered recently is far more troubling than beautiful Dolly's sores. Recently I've been noticing that the caulking that holds the aquarium glass to the cave wall has a crack in it."

"A crack in it?" said Tommy and Jessie as one.

"Yes I'm afraid so," said Hansom. "I'm not sure what it means, but I suspect that it is not good."

THAT NIGHT, LIKE EVERY night, Big Moe slipped out of the aquarium under cover of darkness, his actions focused on a single purpose: helping the crabs grow.

Chapter 12

THE COMMITTEE TO STUDY the warming temperatures did form, but aside from Tommy Tang, Jessie the turtle, and Ally and Altair the seahorses, only Dusty the flounder joined in. Dolly the damselfish and a couple of the grunts initially wanted to be part of it, but when Push and Hammy publically accused them of being "alarmists" they changed their minds, saying they had other things to do. Sanger the squirrelfish said that he would sit in on the meetings but would not participate as he thought the whole thing a waste of time.

Tommy asked Hansom the goatfish to join them, and he said he would. But Tommy noticed that the good doctor seemed to be spending more and more time doing nothing but observing the caulking between the cave wall and the aquarium glass. For quite some time, Hansom missed every meeting.

Sanger's disparaging remarks aside, the committee continued to track the thermometer readings. The temperature came up another degree in the next two weeks. Ally and Altair tried to get the word out to the other creatures. But each time the seahorses said something Push and Hammy were there to yell, "Alarmist nags," and then no one seemed to listen to them anymore.

Mostly the creatures of the aquarium just wanted to eat and be left alone. The Spirulina continued to thrive and aside from some heat discomfort, so did the creatures of the aquarium. True, Dusty's headaches continued and Dolly's sore had not healed. And now four of the wrasses and six of the gobies had an odd white fungus growing on their noses.

HANSOM THE GOATFISH FINALLY came to a committee meeting one day, arriving late. The committee was deep in discussion over their latest temperature observation—up another half degree. Sanger the squirrelfish hovered nearby, a scowl on his face.

"And have you noticed," Jessie the turtle was saying as Hansom swam up, "that more and more of the creatures are spending time in the far corner of the tank, near the bottom, where the cooler ocean water comes in? Seems anymore all most of them do is eat, tend to the algae, then head for the pipe entrance."

"That should be evidence enough to them..." said Altair the seahorse.

"...that the temperature is rising!" finished Ally.

"It seems so apparent," added Tommy Tang, "yet it is beyond me to figure out how we can get the others to understand that we are all in real peril."

That's when Hansom cleared his throat. He gave Sanger a sideways glance as the others turned to face him. "I am sorry to tell you, my friends, that the rising temperature is not our biggest problem."

This direct statement caused them all to pull up short, concern showing in their eyes.

"The crack, Doc," asked Jessie. "Is it the crack between the glass and the cave wall?"

"I'm afraid so," responded Hansom. "The crack is growing a bit each day. I have been taking measurements of it carefully for weeks. What concerns me is that it's not only getting longer, it is getting deeper. I daresay it won't be long until we spring a leak."

"Yes, yes, yes, Hansom." It was Sanger finning forward. "Tommy and Jessie told us about your *great* observation weeks ago. It's nonsense. That crack has been there for as long as I can remember."

In this crowd, Sanger was far outnumbered. The others gave him menacing looks and he retreated.

Hansom tried his best to ignore Sanger and focus on the others. "You all know that Professor Brown caulks the tank yearly. I recall him telling Augustus to keep an eye on just that spot that's cracking."

"As much good as that might do us," said Dusty the flounder.

Hansom nodded thoughtfully, then rubbed his whiskers before continuing. "But here's what I haven't told you. I have been thinking a lot about the rapid expansion of the crack. It seems to be growing so fast. And while yes there have been cracks in the past, that much I will grant to Sanger, this one is like nothing we have seen before."

"So what's going on Doc?" asked Tommy.

"I think, my friends, that your current issue— the increasing temperature—and the rapidly growing crack are related. In fact, I think the increasing temperature is helping dissolve the caulking. You see solvency increases with increasing temperature. That's true for most materials, including the compounds that make up caulking—silicones, polyurethanes, poly..."

"But Doc," Tommy interrupted, "we don't understand. What does that all mean?"

Hansom paused to bite his lip, brow furrowed. When he spoke again, he spoke slowly, "What it means is that we must figure out a way to stop the temperature from rising. If we don't, at the rate the caulking is failing I fear that the seal could break before Professor Brown returns in three weeks."

"Oh my God!" exclaimed Jessie, who alone immediately saw what the good doctor would say next.

"And I am sad to say, my friends, if the caulking seal breaks before the professor returns, the aquarium will likely drain and we will all die."

IN THE COMING WEEK, Tommy Tang and Jessie the turtle swam ceaselessly around the aquarium trying to inform the other creatures of Doc Hansom's research into the cracking of the caulk. They were surprised to get little response. Though the crack was easy enough to see, they found it remarkably difficult to get the others to show any concern. So it leaks a bit, big deal, seemed to be the overriding opinion. Most of the other creatures continued to just want to eat and be left to their own devices in the bottom of the far end of the aquarium, where the cool waters from the incoming pipe entered.

Undaunted, Tommy and Jessie called the creatures together again, this time back at the ledge in the cave wall, just below where the crack in the caulking could be seen.

"I thought the committee was going to get back to us in two or three months," yelled Sarin the crab, before Tommy could even start. "It's not even been a month. Why are you bothering us? We have lives to live."

"Because I wanted everyone together to see the crack in the caulking." Here Tommy motioned to Jessie, floating above at the seam of the cave wall and the aquarium glass. Jessie pointed at the crack for all to see.

"Doc Hansom," said Tommy, "has shown that the crack is growing longer and deeper by the day. If the crack gets big enough it could start to leak."

Here Tommy paused, considering one last time the prudence of revealing Hansom's biggest concern. Then he plowed on: "And Hansom says if the seal breaks that the whole seam might fail, meaning water could rush out of the aquarium killing us all."

Many of the creatures gasped. They'd heard about the crack, of course, but this latest twist caught them by surprise.

"Oh for goodness sake," said Roop, quieting the crowd. "First the temperature, now the *great and scary* crack. Can't you all see that Mr. Tang here, his turtle friend, and that silly old goatfish are just alarmists who want to scare you? It's the only thing that gives them any importance around here!"

"Stargazers!" yelled Push the puffer.

"Whackos!" hollered Hammy the parrotfish.

"Alarmists!" muttered Sanger the squirrelfish.

"Stargazing whacko alarmists! ALARMING WHACKO STARGAZERS!" screamed Flecky the clownfish from the edge of his protected anemone perch.

The shrimp all looked disgusted. One of the shrimp moved to leave and as soon as it started they all departed for work back in the bubble algae patches. Others began to mumble in discord.

But a moment later, Gabe the angelfish suddenly shouted over the chaos, "QUIET DOWN, all of you!" His fierceness caught even his spouse Zuriela by surprise, and she drifted backwards behind him protectively. The crowd quieted, stunned by Gabe's tone.

"What is wrong with all of you?" Gabe continued. "It *is* hot, we can no longer deny it. Every day I listen to all of you complain of the heat, then watch as you huddle in the cool waters at the incoming pipe."

Several of the creatures nodded. One of the grunts grumbled, "True enough."

"And look up there where Jessie is. LOOK! There is a crack there and it is bigger today than when I first saw it no matter what *anyone* tells me." Here Gabe glared at Sarin and Roop and their cronies.

Several heads nodded again. This time it was one of the wrasses who said, "Also true."

"So I say let's hear them out." Gabe stopped. Shouts of agreement rose from the crowd. The crabs huddled together, but said nothing.

Tommy finned forward and said, "Thanks Gabe." Then turning to make room, he said, "Doc, can you fill us in?"

Hansom came forward to provide updated details of his research to the aquarium creatures. Jessie swam down to be at the goatfish's side. The creatures listened attentively and when Sanger tried to interrupt, Dusty the flounder flicked a cloud of silt up to stop him.

"So the worrisome part," Doc Hansom continued, barely noticing the commotion beside him, "is that the caulking is slowly dissolving because of the increased temperatures. If the caulking gives way we might not just have a little leak. Instead I think we are in danger of the entire seal failing catastrophically. I suspect that once part of it goes, it will all go and the aquarium wall might blow out. So, my friends, we *must* do something."

"Put our faith in Professor Brown," said Sarin, interrupting, "he'll be back in two weeks and save us!"

There were grumbles, but Sarin's words picked up no endorsement from the crowd.

Hansom continued, clearly dismissive of Sarin's attempt to change the discussion. "Let me repeat myself, so there is no confusion. If the caulking fails before Professor Brown returns, water will almost certainly rush out of the aquarium, devastating life as we know it."

That thought left the crowd quiet, solemn. Sarin looked livid for being ignored, but said nothing.

In a moment Hansom slipped back, obviously complete with what he wanted to say. Tommy finned up, and said, "Thanks Doc," then turned to the assembled creatures of the aquarium. "The question then, my friends, is what can we do from here? Sarin has given us one option: Let's just do nothing and pray for the best."

Sarin and Roop looked hopefully about at the others, but again no one gave them any heed.

With the silence saying legions, Tommy moved on with the creatures' implicit go ahead. "Or...our committee has come up with two more ideas, things that we can actively do to help ourselves. First, we can try to reseal the caulking with mud from the aquarium bottom. Dusty already volunteered to lead that effort."

"We'll help," said three of the grunts in unison. Gabe and Zuriela also volunteered.

"What else can we do?" asked Dolly the damselfish.

"We need to drop the temperature," Tommy replied, "like Doc said so that the caulking doesn't' degrade so rapidly."

"And how do you propose to do that?" asked Roop caustically.

"Oh never mind," said Sarin. "This is the biggest load of manure I have ever heard. Let's go!" With that Sarin and Roop turned and left. In a few seconds Push, Hammy, and Sanger followed. Big Moe took a couple steps away with departing group, but then stopped on the edge of the crowd and continued to listen.

"To answer Roop," Tommy said, gesturing at the departing group, "we don't know how to drop the temperature because we don't know why the temperature has been rising. We do know, however, that the crack is in the warmest part of the tank. So if we can get some of the cold water channeled over there we just might slow the degradation of the caulk until the professor comes back."

"But how do we get cold water from the incoming pipe across the tank to the crack?" asked the goby mother.

"Jessie figured that one out," said Tommy. "Jessie, why don't you fill everyone in?"

Jessie paddled forward and said, "The committee thought our best shot was to have Push and Hammy fill their big cheeks with cold water, then make shuttle runs across the aquarium and blow the cold water on to the crack. With the two of them having just departed, it's apparent that's not going to happen."

"Doesn't matter," said one of the wrasses. "*We'll* do it. There are lots of us and if we all get together we can shuttle cold water over to the caulking."

"Double that," said the goby mother. "The gobies can help to. We *all* need to chip in for the sake of our little ones!"

THAT NIGHT, AS HE had every night, Big Moe climbed the cave wall and exited the aquarium to turn the thermostat up another tiny notch. But this time after Big Moe had completed his assigned task, he decided to crawl back down into the tank along the caulking seal. There, by the glow of a full moon coming in through the overhead light tube, Big Moe saw a most disturbing sight: beads of water had formed along the caulking on the outside of the glass.

Chapter 13

LIKE BIG MOE, HANSOM the goatfish quickly spotted the droplets forming outside the aquarium. As the word of his observation spread, any lingering doubt the creatures might have had about the gravity of their situation disappeared.

For days the wrasses and gobies filled their mouths with cold water and raced back and forth between the pipe that brought cold ocean water into the aquarium and the cracking seal. Others periodically joined in, but it was schools of wrasses and gobies, moving in tandem, that did the yeomen's work.

At the same time Dusty the flounder, Gabe and Zuriela the angelfish, and the grunts tried to re-seal the caulking between the cave wall and aquarium glass. Dusty and the two angelfish dug the mud from the bottom with their tails, then delivered it into place. The grunts pushed and packed it into the crack as best they could.

For almost a week things looked promising. The cool water or the resealing effort or both seemed to be working. The number of drops had not increased in the six days since the big push to solve the problem began.

ON THE SEVENTH DAY of their efforts, something went wrong, very wrong. The grunts were the first to see it. While packing silt into the corner of the aquarium, a big crack, deeper and wider than anything anyone had seen before, suddenly formed right before their eyes. In a matter of seconds, all their collective work over the past week was ruined.

But worse news came when Tommy, Jessie, and Hansom joined the others to inspect the new crack. Outside the aquarium for the first time they could see a tiny rivulet of water running down the aquarium glass. And also, for the first time ever, something else terribly troubling: as the assembled group watched a single air bubble formed on the inside of the crack, broke loose, and floated up through the water to the surface of the aquarium.

Chapter 14

BIG MOE BEGAN TO question himself the night he saw the beads of water outside the aquarium. He watched with interest during the first day that the others worked on patching the crack. On the second day he took a turn with the grunts packing mud and silt into the crack. For this effort he suffered many negative comments from Sarin, Roop, Push, and Hammy. But Big Moe stayed silent, as per usual, so the others thought it just a passing phase.

It wasn't.

On the third night of the effort to stop the crack, Big Moe stopped adjusting the thermostat. To keep up appearances for Sarin and Roop he still crawled out of the aquarium at night, but when Big Moe got to the thermostat he did not turn it up.

Instead he sat and thought.

Big Moe had never had much occasion to think on his own. All his life he had let others do the thinking; he was bigger on action. But those beads of water had really set him to worry. Something felt drastically wrong.

On the seventh day of efforts to seal the crack— the day they all saw the air bubble form—Big Moe went to find Tommy Tang. He told Tommy about the crabs' long-time ploy. Big Moe was ready for the worst, but also felt great relief in being able to tell someone his dark secret.

Tommy surprised him. Tommy did not yell but after shaking his head gave only a single, short response: "We need to tell Doc Hansom."

They found Hansom talking with Jessie the turtle and the two seahorses. Big Moe told them about how the crabs had acted on the good doctor's words that increasing temperatures would increase the food supply, all else be damned.

"Oh my God!" said Altair. "The crabs..."

"...may have killed us all!" finished Ally.

"Yes, that may be true," said Hansom calmly. "But I would suggest we worry about the crabs later."

"What do we do now, Doc?" asked Jessie, wide-eyed.

As per his habit, the goatfish rubbed his whiskers in thought before he spoke. When Hansom looked up his response was simple: "I think it would prudent for us to have Mr. Big Moe go up and turn down the thermostat."

Chapter 15

BY THE NEXT MORNING, now seven days before Professor Brown was expected to return, the thermostat had been turned down and the creatures of the aquarium knew of the crabs' longtime plot to increase algae production and thus help themselves grow.

The creatures fairly quickly accepted Big Moe into their camp. All of them realized that Big Moe had never been the brains behind the crabs' schemes. He had revealed the crabs' plan, helped with their attempt to repair the crack, and gone up and turned the thermostat back down. Plus the other creatures could clearly see that Sarin, Roop, and their cohorts had quickly turned on Big Moe, ostracizing him any time he approached them.

A number of the creatures—led by Gabe the angelfish and Dusty the flounder—talked about teaching the two crabs a lesson. They formed a posse to confront Sarin and Roop and descended upon them in a corner of the aquarium.

Seeing the crabs surrounded by their big friends, Push the puffer and Hammy the parrotfish, not to mention the brigade of shrimp, was enough for the others to drop the idea of corporal punishment. But a shouting match still ensued.

"You could have killed us by turning up the temperature!" yelled Gabe.

"Quit complaining," hollered Sarin right back.

"But the aquarium seal almost broke because of your selfishness!" returned Dusty.

"You were all better off, too!" screamed Roop, not giving an inch. "The Spirulina grew better at higher temperatures and I never heard any of you complain as you were getting fat!"

The verbal battle might have gone on for hours. But at that moment the creatures of the aquarium received a big surprise that would end their confrontation. For at that very moment, on that seventh day before Professor Brown was scheduled to come back from sabbatical, Augustus came marching down the stairs.

Chapter 16

AUGUSTUS DID TWO THINGS immediately after coming into the room. The first was to take a look around in the aquarium. He quickly satisfied himself that most of the professor's creatures looked well, though thought it curious and a little eerie that they all seemed to be lining up on the other side of the glass watching him. Shaking his head with a frown, Augustus stood up and walked over to inspect the food drum.

"Well look at that, Auggie ol' boy," he said aloud, the frown turning to a smile. "Yer timing is perfect! All the professor's critters in the fish tank look fine and appears they jus' run out o' food. You are a mastah, ol' Auggie, an absolute mastah of timing. That food drum held jus' the right amount of food, jus' like you ciphered it out. And look at ya—no work for a year, jus' collecting money. Auggie ol' boy, ya gotta find yerself another gig like this un soon."

Augustus did not dally. He had come to do one thing and one thing only—return the aquarium to how it had looked when Professor Brown left for Australia. That meant removing the food drum off the hopper and disassembling the scaffolding that he had built to hold the drum. He also had to untie the ropes and pull out the anchor hooks he had placed in the walls and ceiling.

It took Augustus an hour to tear everything down, pick up old food bags off the floor, and make four or five runs up the stairs to remove the materials. After his last big haul, he came back down to the aquarium to survey his work.

"Nice job ol' Auggie," he said to himself in congratulations. "Looks jus' like when the professor lef'. He'll never know that anythin' happened here other than jus' what he asked for. Critters look good, everythin' is cleaned up, even put enough food in the hopper so I don't have to come back this last week."

Augustus stepped onto the first stair to depart then, saying, "Yesiree, youse be a smart ol' cookie, ol' Auggie...." Something suddenly felt amiss, causing Augustus to stop his self revelry for a moment. He looked back to see an empty fish tank; no fish seemed to be swimming anywhere about.

Augustus stepped down for a closer look. In a moment he spotted them. All the creatures seemed to be occupying the corner of the fish tank near where the aquarium glass and the cave wall came together. As he started to wonder what was going on, Augustus noticed a pool of water on the floor for the first time, reaching from the edge of the aquarium to the floor drain.

That's strange, Augustus thought to himself, immediately forgetting the gathering of fish. For a moment he considered looking for a towel to clean up the mess, then decided against it. "That'll dry long before Professor Brown gets back," he said, speaking aloud again.

And with that, Augustus turned back once more and headed up the stairs.

Chapter 17

SIX DAYS LEFT BEFORE Professor Brown returned, then five days, then four. With each day the creatures of the aquarium redoubled their efforts to stop the crack from growing. And each day they could see that their efforts were futile. At best they were slowing the tide; at worst the seal was ready to fail at any moment. Most troubling, the crack now reached from top to bottom, the entire length of the aquarium glass.

By three days before the professor was scheduled to return, a visible stream of water could be seen running down the outside of the aquarium. This was no dribble. This was a running flow. And Hansom the goatfish solemnly noted that if one followed the flow down the glass it ran smoothly until interrupted by a small *upward* gusher that had newly emerged from the corner where the cave, the aquarium glass, and the floor came together.

For days now Big Moe had carried mud and silt down the cave wall and tried to reseal the crack in the caulking from outside the aquarium. Back inside the aquarium the shrimp had joined in, forming a bucket brigade of sorts to move more silt up to the crack. The grunts and the angelfish and Dusty the flounder took the silt and mud and frantically pushed it into the ever-growing crack. But whenever they glanced up and came eye-to-eye with Big Moe across the glass, their shared looks revealed only despair.

By this point the temperature in the aquarium had cooled back to normal. But following advice from Hansom, who said, "Well it couldn't hurt," the wrasses and gobies continued to shuttle cold water back and forth from the ocean pipe inflow to the crack.

All their good efforts aside, water continued to stream down the outside of the aquarium.

Chapter 18

WITH TWO DAYS LEFT before Professor Brown's scheduled return, the creatures made a startling discovery: enough water had drained from the aquarium that the feeding tube no longer reached the aquarium surface.

It was Jessie the turtle that first made this observation. Soon Hansom the goatfish started to the surface to survey the scene. When Sanger the squirrelfish asked if he might join him, Hansom paused momentarily, then shrugged as if to say "Come on, then." The two were silent initially, then began to share a few words as they neared the surface. Soon they were swimming back and forth across the aquarium, Jesse trailing them, engaged in deep discussion.

Eventually Hansom and Sanger came back to the bottom of the aquarium. By now Tommy Tang had assembled most of the creatures at the big ledge in the cave wall. Sarin and Roop even attended. Since Augustus had left, the two crabs had spent most of their time collecting the newly falling fish food, but not once participating in the others' efforts to save the aquarium. And for the first time that any of them could remember, Flecky the clownfish left the cover of his anemone and swam forward unprotected to join the other creatures.

Only Big Moe and Dusty did not come to the meeting. Instead, the other creatures could see the big crab and the flounder frantically packing silt into the crack, one on the outside of the aquarium, the other on the inside.

Tommy did not have to quiet the other creatures. They went immediately silent when he said, "Doc Hansom, Sanger," and then motioned them forward. The goatfish and the squirrelfish swam forward together for the first time anyone could remember, but Sanger stopped short, allowing Hansom to have the stage.

"I fear, my friends, that the news is not good," started Hansom. "In fact, I should say that Sanger and I agree that the situation is dire." At this Sanger nodded in agreement, any hostility between the two apparently forgotten due to the emergency situation.

"Our observations and measurements show that we have crossed a critical threshold. We are now losing water out of the crack faster than it is being replaced by the incoming pipe from the ocean."

There were a number of groans.

"But if we can make it until Professor Brown returns in two days, we shall all be fine," said Sarin from the side. For the briefest moment the crowd's mood lightened, until Sanger finned forward.

"Not actually true," said Sanger, quieting the crab. "First of all, we are still in grave danger of the seal failing catastrophically in the next two days. If that happens the aquarium could empty in a matter of seconds. But there's more. Doc...." Sanger motioned for Hansom to continue.

"Yes, I am sorry to say," Hansom continued, "that Sanger and I have calculated that at the rate it is leaking, there is a good chance the aquarium will now empty before the professor's return, even if a catastrophic failure does not occur."

"It may be," Hansom concluded, "that it is already too late."

IN THE FINAL FULL day before Professor Brown was scheduled to return, Push the puffer and Hammy the parrotfish even joined in shuttling cold water to the crack. Flecky the clownfish resumed hiding in the anemone. Sarin and Roop climbed up to the top of the aquarium, slipped out of the water, and found a wet ledge to sit on and survey the scene.

Chapter 19

AS IT TURNS OUT, it was too late, just as Hansom and Sanger had suggested it might be. On the morning of Professor Brown's return, the crack in the caulking seal suddenly split wide open right under Big Moe's feet. Water rushed out of the gaping crack in such a torrent that it swept the big crab off the perch where he worked.

In an instant the aquarium started to empty. But just as the creatures realized their plight, the entire glass wall, no longer anchored to the cave, gave way and crashed to the floor.

Chapter 20

PROFESSOR BROWN LOOKED DOWN to see nothing but blue ocean. He was flying home, currently somewhere east of Hawaii. I hope that idiot Augustus will be there at the airport, he thought to himself.

The professor's journey had been a successful one. Through a combination of science, diplomacy, and overt advocacy he had saved the seahorse community off the coast of Australia.

But while he had successfully led the fight to stop the oil drilling, the battle had tired him. This is a young man's game, he had realized many times. No more sabbaticals, he thought wearily, no more long travel. Over the last three months he had more and more found himself thinking of the beach cottage and wondering how his fish, crabs, and other critters were doing.

He missed the aquarium.

He also found himself wondering if Augustus had done a good job caring for his creatures. Sure, every time they talked through the year Augustus had assured him that the aquarium was humming along exactly as he had left it. But still the professor had an inherent mistrust of his caretaker that his time in Australia had not shaken.

The professor knew he would only be at ease once he saw for himself that all was well.

ALTHOUGH HE WAS AN hour late, Augustus did pick Professor Brown up at the airport, at a bit past noon. For the entire ride to the coast the hired man described all the work he had done over the past year, not so subtly indicating that a bonus might be in order. Things had gone so well, according to Augustus, that he saw no reason to come inside when he dropped the professor off.

"It's yer time to be home and settle in," Augustus said through the rolled down window of his old truck. "You'll be wanting to check out the fish tank." At this reference, Professor Brown grimaced, but he was so happy to be home he let it pass. "Besides it's getting' late, yer prob'ly tired from the jet ride, and I want to be headin' to my place for dinner," Augustus continued. "Ol' Auggie will come back for his last check later this week." With that he drove off.

Professor Brown dropped his bags in the front entrance to the beach cottage and immediately headed for the stairs down to the aquarium. His heart rate quickened; he felt a sense of great excitement.

For a man his age, Professor Brown practically skipped down the stairs, using his cane and the railing to propel himself forward. But three steps from the bottom he pulled up abruptly—something was terribly wrong! Water covered the floor in front of him two inches deep.

Three more steps brought the professor to the foot of the stairs where he could survey the room. The aquarium was empty!

Shattered remnants of the aquarium covered the floor. Amidst the chunks and shards of glass he saw a dead puffer, and next to it a dead parrotfish. Close by were a squirrelfish, a school of gobies, a flounder, and then his favorite, a beautiful damselfish, all also lifeless.

Professor Brown stepped into the room, face aghast. In front of him was a giant slab of glass, much of the original wall of the aquarium, still partially intact. Underneath, smashed into several pieces, was one of his crabs, the one with the single giant claw.

A step further along and the professor could now see many other creatures scattered among the endless glass shards. There were dead wrasses and grunts, each in their own little group. Two angelfish, apparently stone dead like all the rest, lay side by side.

Professor Brown slumped backwards onto a rickety chair. He cupped his face in his hands as tears welled in his eyes. What had happened to the beautiful world he had created?

For a time the professor sat there, quietly sobbing over the destruction of his life's work. But eventually his mind began to clear. Soon he became aware of a rhythmic sound. He rubbed his eyes clear and saw that against the far side of the cave, what had been one wall of the aquarium, water continued to surge into the room from the incoming pipe.

It quickly dawned on Professor Brown that the ocean waves had continued on as ever, even with the aquarium destroyed. Thus the room should be filling with sea water unless the aquarium sump pump was still working.

The professor got to his feet to go inspect the sump. He worked his way through the broken glass, pushing some of it aside with his cane. As he stepped gingerly over a dead clownfish, the professor saw a movement on the floor. In front of him, moving slowly away, was the small turtle that had so newly come to him shortly before his departure to Australia. The professor gently picked up the creature, bigger now, turned it so they were face-to-face, and said, "My poor friend. I am sorry beyond belief that you have all had to suffer so. I only wish that you could tell me what happened."

As had happened a year earlier, the turtle locked eyes with the professor, giving him an eerie feeling.

Still holding the turtle, the professor turned his gaze back to the sump pump, his initial goal. He could see that as its lowest point, the sump was the only place in the aquarium still holding significant water. Professor Brown decided that he would deposit the turtle there for safe keeping until he could more closely survey the scene and decide what to do next.

The professor climbed into the aquarium, making his way through heaps of drying bubble algae that seemed unfamiliar. He quickly set the thought aside; amid the chaos nothing seemed as it should be.

Professor Brown set his cane down as he kneeled at the edge of the small sump pool. Reaching out to set the turtle down, the professor indeed heard the sump pump gently humming as he had surmised it must be. The only thing amiss, aside from scattered debris in the pool, was that the screen over the outlet pipe had come off.

As Professor Brown watched the turtle paddle away he saw something else that made him gasp, not believing his eyes. But as quickly as the vision appeared it was gone, covered by the foam of the next incoming wave. Kneeling as he was the wave soaked the professor to his thighs, but he did not care. He gently wiped away the foam as the water began to calm.

Slowly the scene in the sump pool cleared and came into focus. Professor Brown's eyes had not been playing tricks on him. There in the bottom of the pool were his two precious seahorses, clearly moving about and apparently well.

As the professor watched the turtle swam forward into the scene, directly facing the two seahorses. So long did they face each other that Professor Brown could not shake the feeling that the three were happily greeting each other.

The professor continued to watch the turtle and the seahorses for some time as he considered what to do next. Finally he reached for his cane and struggled to get back on his feet. At that moment the next ocean surge shot through the incoming pipe, knocking him off balance. The professor fell back against the rugged cave wall, and as he did the wall moved, or so it seemed to him.

Gathering himself, Professor Brown turned to the wall for closer inspection. There for the first time he saw two crabs, retreating into a hollow in the rock wall, both eyeing him warily.

THIRTY MINUTES LATER, PROFESSOR Brown set a goldfish bowl down on the kitchen window sill upstairs. The window looked west out along the basalt inlet his cottage sat on, and then further out from there to the open ocean. In the goldfish bowl were the two seahorses, plus a single piece of broken coral the professor had salvaged from the aquarium.

It had been a strange choice, the goldfish bowl, but one that seemed right for the moment when he found it downstairs. The destruction of his aquarium had been so complete, so total, that the professor had only wanted to escape the downstairs as quickly as possible.

Turning away from the goldfish bowl, Professor Brown stooped to pick up a box, then opened the back door. As he walked away from the cottage, the seahorses swam to the edge of the goldfish bowl, looking west toward the ocean.

At that moment the sun was low to the horizon, coloring the sky orange. The sea was strangely calm; barely a ripple covered the glassy surface of the inlet.

The seahorses watched as just a few steps from the ocean Professor Brown stopped, set the box down at his feet, and opened the lid. Quickly two crabs scrambled out the top of the box and then raced across the basalt toward a large tide pool. The crabs paused momentarily at the water's edge to team up and chase off a smaller crab. Then, as quickly as they had arrived at the tide pool, the crabs slipped under its inky water and disappeared.

The seahorses' gaze returned to Professor Brown, whom they could tell had also been watching the crabs. They saw the professor stoop down and carefully remove a turtle from the box. Ever so gingerly the professor stepped to a lower level in the rock, so that he was now standing just a foot above the calm ocean waters. They saw him turn the turtle toward himself, and could see him saying something aloud.

In the next moment the professor leaned out over the water, and then he gently deposited the turtle in the sea.

In Gratitude

MANY EARLY READERS HAD an impact on *FISH TANK*, and hence on my vision for the book, and I would like to express my great appreciation to them. The book's shortcomings are mine; its strengths emanate from the collective community of friends and family who set aside some of their valuable time to help me.

More than a few issues came to light during the reviews, not the least being that in an early version of the book I had included both fresh and salt water fish in the same aquarium. That mistake would have surely stretched readers' willingness to suspend disbelief with me a bit too far!

It truly did take a community to create this book. Core to that community, to *my* community, is my wife and best friend, Katie Gibson, who is instrumental in review, direction, and creativity for all that I do. I thank you with all my heart.

And to so many others who graciously gave of their valuable time, I want to thank you all. Thanks for your insights into and enthusiasm for *FISH TANK* and the story it seeks tell. Thanks to (and my apologies if I miss anyone) Conrad Anker; Linda Ashkenas; Bill Bert Baker; Hattie Baker; Betty Bischke; Chris Boyer; Kathy and Max Brewer; Betsy Buffington; Susan Buhlman; Peter Cook; Pete, Chris, Henry, and Nina Coppolillo; Bob Crabtree; Deb and Lucy Davidson; Kent Davis; Bob and Bonnie Eichenberger; Joan and Tessie Exley; Liz Garton; Giff and Ellen Gibson; Lu Goodrum; Bob Gresswell; Johnna Hietala; Susie, Dennis, and Brittney Iverson; Louise Johnson; Nancy Jordheim; Alan Kesselheim; Gwen Laurie; Annie Lee; Janet Lindsley; Mike Mahoney; Kelly Matheson; Chris Mehl; Natalie Meyer; Julia Olson; Bob Ouradnik; Jody Ouradnik; Raina Plowright; Otto Pohl; Jodie Rein; Steve Running; Chris and Celia Slater; Stuart Vandel; Tom Vandel; Cathy Whitlock; and Kate Wright.

Scott Bischke

Author Bio

SCOTT BISCHKE SERVED AS the Science Writer for the Montana Climate Assessment (2017; see montanaclimate.org). He helped develop the city of Bozeman Municipal Climate Action Plan (task force co-chair, 2008) and Bozeman Community Climate Action Plan (task force member, 2011).

Along with these efforts, Scott's professional life has touched broadly on issues of resource management and climate change. He worked as a chemical engineering researcher at three national laboratories, as an environmental engineer for Hewlett-Packard, as the lab director for the Yellowstone Ecological Research Center, and currently as a science writer and facilitator specializing in Greater Yellowstone Area science and technology issues. As part of those professional

efforts, Scott has led programs for materials
reduction and recycling for major manufacturing
facilities, helped draft research plans and science
agendas dealing with natural resource constraints and
climate change, and completed engineering projects
and served on an electronics industry technical
advisory board scoped at reducing global warming
gases from wafer fabrication processes.

Scott has published four other books, one
fiction, three non-fiction[1]:

o *TRUMPELSTILTSKIN — A Fairy Tale* (MountainWorks Press
  2016);
o *GOOD CAMEL, GOOD LIFE — Finding Enlightenment One Drop
  of Sweat at a Time* (MountainWorks Press 2010);
o *CROSSING DIVIDES — A Couples' Story of Cancer, Hope, and
  Hiking Montana's Continental Divide* (American Cancer
  Society 2002); and
o *TWO WHEELS AROUND NEW ZEALAND —
  A Bicycle Journey on Friendly Roads* (Pruett Publishing
  hardback 1992; Ecopress paperback 1996).

Scott lives with his spouse and best friend, Katie
Gibson, in Bozeman, Montana. The couple has
hiked, biked, and canoed in places far and wide,

---

[1] Find Scott and his books on Amazon, Goodreads, and Facebook, or at
www.scottbischke.com. A *FISH TANK* discussion guide for
classrooms and book clubs can be downloaded at the website, or
found embedded in one version of the book. Kindle and other eBook
formats are available at online stores.

including backpacking the length of the Continental Divide from Canada to Mexico, and hiking and canoeing the length of the Yellowstone River. A common thread in all of Scott and Katie's travels has been their desire to immerse themselves in the peace, solitude, and tranquility of the natural world. The couple seeks out people, places, and activities that reinforce their desire to live a life filled with positive energy. Perhaps more simply, they seek to live a life that reflects their gratitude for being alive each and every day.

Made in the USA
San Bernardino, CA
26 February 2020